SPITFIRE

EVAN BALKAN

SPITFIRE

EVAN BALKAN

tpg

Treehosue Publishing Group | St. Louis, MO

tpg

Published in the United States by Treehouse Publishing Group.
Treehouse is an imprint of Amphorae Publishing Group LLC.
4168 Hartford Street, Saint Louis, MO 63116

This is a work of fiction. Any resemblance to actual events or locales or
persons, living or dead, is merely coincidental, and names, characters,
places, and incidents are either the products of the author's imagination
or are used fictitiously.

"Strange Fruit" was a poem written by Abel Meeropol in
1937 and popularized by singer Billie Holiday.
The poem is in the public domain.

For information, visit us at www.amphoraepublishing.com
Cover art and design by Elena Makansi
Interior layout by Kristina Blank Makansi and Roshni Choudhary

Library of Congress Control Number: 2018950009
ISBN: 9781732139107

For all of the many Towsontowne Tigers who I got to know, love, coach, and play with over the years. But most especially to my two real-life spitfires, Amelia and Molly.

EVERYTHING WAS THE SAME where Caroline Panski lived. All the streets in her neighborhood were the same. The rows upon rows of brick houses were the same, with the same windows and the same marble stoops. It had always been the same, and it always would be the same. There weren't even any trees to break up the monotony. At twelve years old, Caroline was old enough to know that as long as she was stuck in her boring Highland-town neighborhood in boring old Baltimore, nothing would ever change. And, therefore, nothing would ever be any fun.

Inside the modest Panski home on South Clinton Street, Caroline sat in the cramped space afforded by the bow window and stared at the steady diet of rain and sleet outside. If only it would snow, she thought.

Behind her, a clamor of mundane domestic noises competed with the radio: "It's twenty-seven degrees Fahrenheit in Baltimore on this, the second day of December, 1952. Rain continues." There followed a blast of tinny music, followed by a deep, serious voice: "Now, Edward R. Murrow and the voices of President Harry S. Truman, Bernard F. Baruch, Senator Robert Taft, General George C. Marshall, Governor Earl Warren, and more than forty other men and women in this evening's performance of *Hear it Now* presented tonight, and every week, at this time. Later, an editorial. Children in Asia are dying of starvation and the bestselling books in America are how to get thin. But first, we go to the cold battlefields of Korea, where our brave American fighting men—"

Always on alert for news from Korea, Caroline tried to block out everything but the voice on the radio. But like usual, Eloise

Panski switched off the radio and called out to her daughter from the kitchen.

"Caroline? Have you completed your studies?"

"Mm-hmm."

Mrs. Panski, moving with a slight limp, appeared in the doorway and scrutinized Caroline. "You can't go out in this mess again."

Caroline continued staring out the window, watching as two boys engaged in some rough horseplay out on the sidewalk as they passed. "I know."

"Not while it's sleeting."

Mrs. Panski regarded her daughter and uttered a slight sigh of exasperation. "Supper in one hour," she said before retreating to the kitchen where the symphony of clanging pots and pans resumed.

Beautiful, their decrepit miniature schnauzer, padded up to Caroline and nudged her leg. Caroline reached down and reflexively scratched Beautiful behind the ear. As she stared out the window, what had begun as a barely perceptible change slowly became visibly noticeable—the sleet was turning to fat snowflakes. Caroline's eyes brightened. She gave Beautiful one last pat on the head and tore away, sending the dog scurrying for cover under a nearby chair.

Caroline hit the narrow stairs running, squeezing past her seven-year-old-brother along the way.

"Hey! Watch it!" Sam yelled.

She ignored him and bounded into her tiny bedroom. She reached into the closet and pulled out a pair of ice skates, laces tied together, and flung them over her shoulder. Next to the closet, a hockey stick leaned against the wall. She grabbed this, too, and started to run out of her room. But she paused, looking at the picture of the handsome man in an Army uniform that rested on her dresser. She smiled at it, then took off again, down the stairs, through the front door, and into the snow.

It was coming down harder now, the snow-flakes unrelenting, sticking to everything in sight. With little regard for the slippery conditions, Caroline barreled down the street, tore through an alley, and emerged onto an abandoned lot. Surrounded on all sides by crowded rows of dilapidated houses, like cracked teeth chattering in the freezing weather, sat a large semicircle of frozen water, a temporary pond in a world of glass and brick and concrete.

Caroline plopped down into the snow, pulled off her boots, and laced up her skates. She raced out onto the ice and executed a perfect spin. She skated and skated, warming herself up. Not without a few stumbles but with a certain beauty and competence, as if on the edge of skating greatness. The coiled up tension of her athleticism bubbled forward, propelling her from one end of the pond to the other, legs pumping, making quick work of the rough uneven surface.

She stopped, set her sights on the far end of the pond, and raced in that direction as quickly as she could, her breath trailing behind in little puffs and plumes. Racing, skating, racing …

until she tripped over a rock and sprawled headfirst onto the ice with an *oomph*! Caroline pushed herself up, wiped the ice crystals from her coat, and ran her mitten over her chin. She looked at her mitten and frowned at the smeared droplets of blood.

She scowled at the offending rock before straightening and speeding over to where she'd left her hockey stick by her boots. She came to an abrupt stop, spraying ice and snow on her boots, grabbed the stick, and took off back across the ice.

Her hands deftly cradled the stick, switching back and forth, letting it slide and bump over the icy surface until she reached the rock. Without breaking stride, she made contact and pushed the rock along the ice, racing and pushing, moving her way across the pond until she slowed, veered to the right, pushed the rock ahead, and then wound up and let loose a mean slapshot toward the crude net someone had set up to approximate a hockey goal. The rock skipped off the ice, shuttling through a hole in the netting and slamming into the rusted hood of an abandoned car.

"Goal!" Caroline raised her stick high in triumph. She smiled at the cartoon figure imprinted on the wood and then brought it to her lips. This was as close as she could get to her father. He'd given her the stick years earlier. And now, it was like he was here, watching her, encouraging her, skating alongside her instead of fighting on some frozen battlefield on the other side of the world.

Caroline shut the door behind her and stomped the snow off her boots. She looked up when she felt her mother staring at her from the kitchen doorway.

"Supper's ready. I've been calling."

Caroline, red cheeked and still breathing hard, brushed a strand of wet hair out of her eyes. "It stopped sleeting. It's just snow."

"I know, but I told you I don't like you running off like that without telling me. Now get out of those wet things and get cleaned up."

Caroline shed her wet coat and pants, the cuffs of which were caked with snow, and dropped them on the rug. Then she plucked up her skates and stick and ran up the stairs, twirling around the banister and skipping into her bedroom. She was a swirl of activity, tossing her skates and her stick in the corner near her closet, changing into dry clothes, and running a brush through her wet hair. But then she stopped and moved to her dresser. She picked up the picture of her father in his army uniform and rubbed her fingers across it.

"Caroline!"

"Coming."

Caroline took the stairs two at a time and slid into her seat at the table where her mother and brother already sat with hands folded in their laps. Mrs. Panski lowered her head.

"We give thanks for these our gifts—" Sam looked up and stuck his tongue out at his sister.

Caroline lifted a hunk of mashed potatoes in her fingers and threatened to fire it at her brother. "—through the bounty of Christ our Lord."

Caroline sucked the potatoes from her fingers and swallowed hard before her mother looked up.

"Amen."

"Amen."

They made the sign of the cross and then Caroline dug in with unrestrained vigor.

"Caroline, really!" Mrs. Panski protested, her eyes wide in horror. "A lady should have manners."

Caroline shot a sideways glance at Sam as he shoveled food into his mouth without a care in the world. But she didn't say anything. It wouldn't do any good anyway. Boys were boys. Girls were girls. And girls should have manners.

After dinner, Caroline retreated to her bedroom, thankful for the millionth time that she no longer had to share a room with Sam.

Thankful that her dad had understood how important it was for her to have her own space. She remembered when he'd first suggested that he clear out his storeroom as a present for her tenth birthday. "There's too much junk in here anyway," he'd said. "Time for you to have your own room."

He'd sorted through old boxes, carted stuff to the basement, gifted a few things to neighbors, and eventually ended up with two boxes of worthless stuff that he and Caroline had hauled off to the dump. First they'd taken the Roland Park trolley line and then the public bus all the way past Towson and into the suburban hinterlands north of Timonium, a scarred landscape of ex-farmland with patterns of foundations for new subdivisions. She remembered the look on her father's face, the way he watched as the bus traveled north along York Road, passing the construction workers spreading the tentacles of civilization in the age of the automobile, an age of mobility. Perhaps someday, his face seemed to say.

She missed him, terribly. She was just like him—at least that's what everyone said. Not only did she look like him—with the same long, dark eyelashes atop icy blue eyes—but they shared a certain outlook on the world as well, a way of willfully failing to understand things that inconvenienced them. It was this same attribute that allowed her to not worry endlessly about him. When she did think about him, it hurt too much. Baltimore was cold, but Korea, she understood, was worse.

She knew better than to consult her geography textbook again. She'd made that mistake once. *Roddy's Elementary Geography* was an old textbook, many of the maps out of date, but her class at school still used it. When she'd looked up the section with Korea in it, she'd learned very little. But this was, apparently, by design. The book said: "Like China, Korea has had little to do with foreign nations and people. It is often called the 'Hermit Nation'."

This sense of mystery produced a foreboding in Caroline. Just what kind of a place had he been sent to? It was difficult to find out. The entry went on to say that, "The people resemble the Chinese." That was a terrifying prospect, for, according to Roddy's,

The Chinese have many curious customs and ideas. The higher classes bandage the feet of their girls so as to prevent growth. They think small feet very beautiful, even though the feet are terribly deformed and can hardly be used for walking.

She'd pictured an army of little girls and women hobbling along on tiny club feet. Did her dad see women like that and think longingly of his own girl, back home in Baltimore, stuffing her intact and growing feet into hockey skates? Or did the Koreans even do this? They "resembled" the Chinese, but what did that mean exactly? It was all so confusing.

Better to not think about it. Better to picture him with some of the comforts of home. Better to imagine him getting warmed by a fire or, even better, inside a building, drinking coffee and laughing with his fellow soldiers. Yes, that's how she thought of him. It wasn't so hard to do when she forced herself. And so with the occasional inevitable lapse and accompanying tears, she more or less went through her days keeping her father and Korea and war locked away in the recesses of her thoughts.

Caroline turned toward the window and peered outside. The snow continued to fall, but lighter now. She slid open her window, her breath pluming in front of her, and twisted her body, straining, until, in the far distance, she could see the pond. There, a dozen boys played hockey, barely lit by ambient gaslight. Even at this distance, she could tell they were skilled players, executing difficult moves, and firing the puck with great speed and force. She could almost feel her fingers tighten around her stick. Oh, how she wished she was on the ice now!

Hearing someone coming, Caroline quickly closed the window and threw herself onto her bed just before her mother entered.

"Lights out," she said. She looked around, her brow furrowed. "Why is it so cold in here?"

"But it's only 8:30," Caroline protested.

"Be grateful you have a roof over your head and food to eat. Did you hear the program about the starving Asian boys and girls?"

"Is that what Daddy is doing there? Helping those boys and girls get food?"

Mrs. Panski got her look again. "Can we talk about this another time?"

"But that's what you always say."

"Good night, Caroline."

"Mama?"

"Yes, Caroline?"

"Do little girls in Korea have to have their feet bandaged?"

"What do you mean?"

"So that their feet are really small? Like the Chinese?"

"I don't have any idea what you're talking about." Mrs. Panski snapped off the lights. "Good night."

"Good night, Mama."

14

Caroline waited a moment and then returned to the window. Without opening it and leaning out, she could only see a small part of the pond, but she knew the boys were still there. She watched for a few minutes and saw their dark, hulking shadows slide across the ice and then disappear again. Then she turned away and slipped into bed.

2

BRIGHT SUNLIGHT GREETED Caroline as she crawled out from under her blankets. She looked outside at a world covered in white, and squinted. A man swept snow from the windshield of his car, a lonely fruit seller prodded his horse, laden with snow bells and pulling an empty cart along the street, and a bus whooshed past, washing the world in a fine, white spray.

Caroline could hear the sounds of breakfast being prepared downstairs and then the familiar call: "Caroline, get dressed for school and come down to eat. You're late."

She raced through her breakfast and then headed out. On the sidewalk, her friend Alma waited.

"Come on," Alma said. "Mustn't keep Bee waiting. You know how she gets."

The two girls hurried along the sidewalk and were soon joined by two more friends, Beatrice and Genevieve. Each of the girls wore essentially the same uniform: knee-length skirts, white socks pulled up to their knees, snow boots, heavy winter coats with fur-lined collars, and knitted caps.

Beatrice piped up, "What took you so long?"

"Sorry," Caroline said as the four girls resumed their march along the sidewalk, kicking at shoveled snow mounds along the way.

"I hope Miss Bloom is sick today," Alma said. "Or fell in the snow and can't get up."

Genevieve shuddered. "I don't think witches can get sick."

Caroline tsked. "That's mean."

"Caroline gave Miss Bloom an apple on the first day," Genevieve said, employing a sing-song voice which she used frequently.

"Too bad it wasn't poisoned," Beatrice added.

Caroline rolled her eyes.

"Little Caroline, always defending Miss Bloom. Face the facts, Caroline, the woman is undoubtedly and indisputably a witch."

"Un-what?" Alma asked.

Genevieve rolled her eyes. "Try reading some books, Alma."

"Who needs books when you have a television?"

Caroline winced. "Puhleeeeeeze tell me we don't have to listen to you go on about that television again."

"Last night, we watched Groucho Marx and *Your Show of Shows*."

At the crossing, the girls kept up their chatter, looking both ways for cars and buses. Caroline craned her head and, through an alley, could just see the edge of the frozen hockey pond. A couple of geese waddled across the surface, taking small ungainly leaps into the air and coming to rest on top of the rusted automobile where Caroline had sent her rock puck.

"Caroline!"

When Caroline looked up, she saw Beatrice, hands on her hips, staring at her in exasperation. The girls were already on the sidewalk and a car sat waiting patiently in the middle of the road for Caroline to join them. She waved at the driver and hurried across the street as a stream of students shuffled into school.

Miss Bloom moved to the blackboard where a map of China and the Korean peninsula were displayed. She was a portly, no-nonsense woman in her late fifties who wore her hair pulled into a severe bun and sported cat-eye glasses attached to a chain around her neck.

"This is the line where our brave American men are fighting the fascist, communist forces of Mousy Tongue," she said. "Class, what is the difference between Americans and Communists?"

Caroline stared out the window and wondered if she'd be able to sneak over to the pond before dinner as Anthony, a humorless kid with brilliantined hair, waved his hand in the air. "The communists are godless, ma'am."

"Very good, Anthony. And we will win in Korea just as we won on the battlefields of Europe and the Pacific. Because God is on the side of the United States of America."

Caroline hoped she wouldn't have too much homework. Her mother wouldn't let her skate if she didn't get her work done first.

"Miss Panski!" Miss Bloom bellowed.

Caroline snapped to attention. "Yes, ma'am?"

"I was reminding the class that your brave father, a God-fearing man I am certain, is on the cold battlefields of Korea. Isn't that right?"

"Yes, ma'am."

"We owe a debt of gratitude to soldiers like your father. It's because of men like him that we can enjoy the freedoms we have here today. Now let's practice our air raid drill."

The students threw their books and papers into their desks. A siren sounded, and they all dropped to the floor and scurried under their desks. Alma and Genevieve had an unobstructed view of one another. They stuck out their tongues and made silly faces, pausing only when Miss Bloom's thick, stockinged legs waddled past.

Caroline didn't see them. Instead, she stared at the ground. While her father was never too far from her thoughts, and she knew Miss Bloom meant well, she was sorry that her teacher had talked about him to the whole class. It brought back that old familiar feeling deep in the pit of her stomach, the one that threatened to make her sick with worry. She hated it.

One tear weaved its way down her cheek. It traced a path along the cut still visible on her chin. She quickly wiped it away.

When the school bell rang at the end of the day, the children burst out the front doors. The boys immediately made for the snow piles. They grabbed handfuls of snow and threw them at one another as the girls dodged and ran as quickly as they could out of the line of fire.

Once clear and on the shoveled sidewalk, Caroline, Alma, Beatrice, and Genevieve walked toward home together. As they passed the high school, they noticed a small crowd milling around, looking agitated. One man held a sign that read, "Race Mixing is Communism". Another sign read, "Cursed is the Man who Integrates," and a woman in a bright blue coat and matching hat waved a sign with big block letters that read, "Go Back to Africa."

Caroline stopped and turned to her friends. "I wonder what's going on."

"I think it's because we're going to have Negroes in our school," Alma said. "They call it 'integer' or something."

"Where'd you hear that?"

Alma shrugged. "My parents. They thought I was in bed, but I was sitting at the top of the stairs so I could hear what they were talking about. My dad was pretty upset."

"Upset about what?"

"We'll, he's against it." Alma shook her fist in the air and scrunched her face up to imitate her father. "Those niggers will come to our schools over my dead body. They got their own schools. Why the heck they have to come to ours?' With a laugh, she let her fist drop. "Course, he didn't say 'heck'."

Caroline shook her head. "I don't see what the big deal is. Negroes in school. So what?"

"They're just different from us, is all."

Beatrice stared at the signs for a moment and then turned to Alma. "Frankly, I think your parents are right. Why do they need to come to our schools when they have their own?"

"'All men are created equal', Genevieve said and started walking, leading the group past the protesters. "I read that somewhere."

"But Negroes aren't as smart as white people. How will they keep up in class?"

"That's a bunch of hogwash," Genevieve protested. "Some people say Jews are greedy, and that's stupid, too. Mr. Rosenbaum gives me free treats every time me and my mom go in his grocery store."

Alma kicked at a pile of snow. "All I know is that they're really funny. That Ethel Waters in *Beulah*. As 'queen of the kitchen,' she's great. And Amos and Andy."

Genevieve shook her head. "But those people aren't even real."

"On the television show they are," Alma protested.

Genevieve rolled her eyes. "Again with the television."

"You're just jealous you don't have one," Beatrice chimed in.

"I can't deny that," Genevieve said with a laugh.

"Well, I just hope none of them try to come to our school." Beatrice pulled her hat down over her ears as the girls continued on until they reached the place where Beatrice and Genevieve would head one direction and Alma and Caroline would head another.

"Have fun at piano practice," Alma said before the group split up.

"Ick," Genevieve replied. "I've barely practiced all week."

"Have a stupendous time doing whatever you two do on Tuesday afternoons," Beatrice said.

"We will," Alma said with a crisp nod. "Indis ... uh ... Indisputablebly."

Beatrice shook her head sadly. "Really, Alma. A book. Try it sometime."

"Not tonight. *Webster Webfoot*'s on—he's my favorite."

And with that, the pairs said goodbye and went their separate ways.

"You really think we'll have Negroes in our school someday?" Caroline asked after they'd turned a corner.

Alma shrugged. "Beats me."

"Well, like I said, I just don't see the big deal. They have a right to an education, too."

"Well, this is me." Alma skipped up the steps of a rowhouse and disappeared inside with a wave, leaving Caroline to continue on her way until she reached her own house.

"I'm home!" she hollered when she stepped inside. A few moments later, Sam appeared, twirling a pinwheel.

"Mom's next door, at the Knudsens."

Caroline absorbed this information for a beat and then raced upstairs. She came bounding back moments later, skates over her shoulder and hockey stick in hand, and bolted toward the front door.

"Hey!" Sam yelled. "Mom said you're supposed to help me with my school work."

Caroline was halfway out the door, but managed to declare, "Do it yourself," before she sprinted outside, where she turned left. When she came to the Knudsen's, a few doors down, she crouched low and skirted past the front stoop, trying to keep from being spotted. As soon as she passed, she took off again, peeling off at the first alley. Caroline emerged from the alley and stopped short.

On the frozen pond, a dozen or so young

boys had already started a game. They were skating roughly, playing with abandon as hip checks sent a few of them teetering across the ice. A few high sticks threatened teeth.

But then she inhaled deeply, gathering her resolve. Slowly, she made her way over. The boys continued playing—until one by one they noticed her. They stopped, each holding his stick across his knees. It had the feel of a showdown: twelve boys on one side, Caroline on the other, each waiting for the other to do something. Finally, one boy, a kid name Alan, skated forward.

"You lost? What do you want?"

Caroline didn't answer.

Another boy spoke up. "You dumb or somethin'?"

A third kid, gangly and awkward even without ice skates, added, "Look, guys: It's Sonja Henie," cracking himself up.

The other boys laughed, too. Gangly, encouraged now by the others, continued, "This ain't Rockefeller Center, sweetheart."

"You can't figure skate today," another said. "We got the ice. You can go over to Carlin's, little girl."

"Or Patterson Park—that's where girls skate."

Caroline stood her ground. "I don't want to figure skate," she said. "I want to play hockey."

The boys burst out laughing, as if this was the most hysterical thing they'd ever heard.

"Girls figure skate," the first boy snorted. "Boys play hockey. Now get outta here. Go on over to Patterson Park and let us get back to our game."

"But they don't let you play hockey in Patterson Park," Caroline said.

This prompted more laughter. "Well, we're not gonna let you play hockey here, either!" one of the boys shouted. Caroline stared at them for a moment longer, but they were already skating away, returning to the chaos of their game. Her fingers gripped her stick as she turned and walked away, eyes burning.

The boys' mention of Carlin's especially

stung because that had been where her father first took her out on the ice. It was a destination like no other, and she remembered her parents talking about it when she was little, like it was some mythical wonderland, a crazy place where anything could happen. Days at Carlin's constituted her father's earliest memories, and he often told Caroline and Sam about those zany times, when pole-sitting, for some reason, was all the rage. Back in '29, when the famous "Shipwreck" Kelly came to Carlin's and sat on top of a platform on a little pole for forty-five days and nights. He even slept up there, and bathed, too, using wet rags. "Well, how did he go to the bathroom?" Sam asked and Mrs. Panski shushed him for his interest in such things, despite the fact that both Caroline and Mrs. Panski herself giggled at the question.

"He was allowed five minutes off the pole every day," Mr. Panski answered.

"So he had to hurry," Sam said.

Again, giggles all around.

"It was a whole craze. After Shipwreck Kelly was here, kids all over the city started climbing into trees and wouldn't come down."

"Did you do that, Daddy?"

"Shoot. Your granddaddy would have skinned me alive if I tried that."

"But there was that one kid—" Mrs. Panski added.

"A.C. Forman. He went up for ten days. Even the mayor came and stood below the pole, passing out business cards."

Caroline would watch wordlessly as they reminisced, enthralled by her parents' memories, when they lived an unfettered life, a time before she and Sam, a time when they first fell in love. And they were in love still. Caroline could tell when they'd both go on about Carlin's. Caroline would just watch them, smiling an unembarrassed smile as her mother and father laughed uncontrollably, stopping to touch one another on the hand, her dad having trouble getting through the famous referee story while her mom wiped away tears of mirth. Upon Caroline and Sam's prompting, her dad would tell it again and again as if it was the first, and not the twentieth, time he'd told it. The one about old Ed Brockman—he was the referee—when his trousers split right down the middle. It was a wrestling match between Ray Steele and George Zaharias. "He was married to the great athlete Babe Didrikson," Mrs. Panski put in. "Yes, yes, the Babe's husband. And there they were, grappling with each other, and old Brockman's trousers … right down the middle."

Mr. Panski got up, bowed his legs, demonstrating, to Caroline's absolute delight. "Someone in the audience threw a pair of lavender bloomers…" Here, Caroline's parents absolutely lost it, falling all over each other with laughter. "And Brockman put them on. The sight of that man throwing himself between the wrestlers wearing those bloomers. I'll never forget it." They could hardly breathe by this time in the story. "Steele and Zaharias themselves were laughing so hard they could hardly stand up." Her parents eventually got control of themselves, sighing in remembrance of being young and in love.

Yes, Carlin's. First it was just stories. But then an actual visit. The wonderful build up, in late winter or early spring, the tension rising for a late summer present before Caroline started school in the fall. When she finally got to actually go, she just couldn't believe it.

From the moment she arrived and saw the twin towers flanking the entrance, she realized that, even in her wild imaginings, she had underestimated its grandeur, and these imaginings had derived from her father's breathless remembrance of the first time he'd been there, as a little tike in the 1920s, when he saw Shipwreck Kelly and all that. In fact, he still held on to a souvenir of that time, a small poster he kept rolled up in a box in the basement. He'd shown it to her, its promise of "Continuous Dancing" to the music of the "Famous Louisiana Five and Mata's Tropical Marimba Band" in addition to the "Colossal Midway," the "Tokio Gardens," "wonderful exhibitions in the magnificent Ice Palace," and, in big bold letters that seemed to burst forth from the page: "Stupendous Display of Gorgeous Fireworks."

The three of them had gone together, before Sam was born, and so Caroline had both of her parents all to herself. She rode the airplane ride, watching the blur of Park Heights Avenue zip by, watching her mother and father's beaming faces flash by as she swirled round and round. She rode the teacups, too, giggling every time she whipped in a little circle.

Her father showed his prowess at the rifle range, hitting every swinging target and presenting Caroline with a stuffed teddy bear for his marksmanship. "Fine work, sir," the attendant told him as he handed the bear to Caroline. She took it in her hands, squeezed it, and clutched it to her side virtually nonstop. For years afterward, it enjoyed a prominent spot at the foot of her bed.

There were the swinging chairs which made her scared, nauseous, and brought on a torrent of tears, something ultimately salved by an ice cream cone. In the distance loomed the gargantuan roller coaster, of which they steered clear. But the big draw seemed to be roller skating. All around town you could see posters exhorting you to "make a date to roller skate at Carlin's." By the time the day ended, Caroline was in her father's arms, desperately trying to keep her eyes open as she watched with a mixture of fascination and envy a line of boisterous teenagers heading toward the coliseum for an all-night dance contest. The last she could remember seeing was a beautiful young woman, probably seventeen or so, wearing a long billowy skirt and holding a pair of roller skates, entering the park just as the Panskis were leaving. The excitement of that: to be just starting your evening as theirs was ending. She couldn't wait to grow up, to be out late, to do whatever she wanted to do. It was, up to that point, the most thrilling day of her young life.

But they didn't go back to Carlin's for a long time after. Her mother told her they didn't have the extra money, especially after Sam arrived. Yet one more reason to loathe her brother. In fact, Mrs. Panski told her in no uncertain terms, after Caroline had asked for probably the tenth time if they could go back, she better stop asking because it wasn't fair to Sam to have to hear about an event that he did not partake in and that he couldn't experience or enjoy now.

And then their luck changed when Mrs. Panski opened her loaf of White's Big Tip-Top Bread to find two free tickets "for the LEADING AMUSEMENTS at Carlin's Liberty Heights Park."

Then things went from lucky to downright miraculous. Mr. Panski came home that very evening clutching two tickets to Carlin's he'd won at a raffle at work. So the family, never giving one thought to returning to Carlin's when they woke that morning, had four tickets by sundown.

It was a different place when they returned, but no less exhilarating. Still billed as "Clean Fun for the Entire Family," the roller coaster and teacups and swings were still there, but there were new rides, too. There were also circus acts, live bands, even operas. That, and ice skating. Caroline found it a bit odd why her mother didn't skate with them but rather sat outside the rink watching Caroline and her dad. Perhaps Sam needed attending to, but Caroline didn't ask. She was too busy holding on to her father's fingers as he led her onto the ice. He wasn't terribly steady himself out there, but he knew enough to keep himself upright and to act as support for her as she took small, chopping steps, clutching on to his forearms and elbows when she threatened to spill. He held on to her no less tightly and no less securely than those moments when he'd come home from work and she'd meet him out on the sidewalk, hopping down the stoop and flinging herself into the air, knowing he'd catch her, that he would never let her fall.

There was a winter carnival going on with top flight ice skaters performing. Caroline enjoyed this, but she was absolutely enthralled with the next event, a hockey game between the Baltimore Clippers and the Cleveland Knights of the Eastern Amateur Hockey League. Sam was yawning and whining by the end of the first period and the Panskis lasted only until the middle of the second period, but Caroline's obvious disappointment over leaving was pacified when her dad, sucker for his crestfallen daughter, promised they'd come back, just the two of them, to see another game one day soon.

True to his word, and after a few extra overtime shifts, he took Caroline to a game between the Clippers and the Atlantic City Seagulls. The whole atmosphere was electric—hundreds of fans in their seats, screaming and spilling their beer under banners hanging from the ceiling proclaiming the league champion Orioles teams of 1934, 1936, and 1940. Her dad told her that the Orioles had folded but that the Clippers were the new team now, and "they'll win the championship this year. You can bet on that." And sure enough they did, breaking the Boston Olympics' streak of four straight titles.

But all of that paled in comparison to what happened after the game, a 6-2 Clippers victory. As part of a promotion, all kids under fourteen were allowed on the ice. The players showed them how to hold a stick and how to shoot a puck. One of the Clippers, a 6'4 bruiser missing four of his teeth, handed Caroline his stick. She could hardly lift it, but he positioned himself behind her, helped her wheel it back and wind up. Together, they let fly a spinning beauty that saucered into the upper right corner of the goal. That had been special enough. But the evening wasn't done. Mr. Panski had another surprise.

Giddy and beaming, he tapped Caroline's shoulder as they were leaving the rink, crooked a finger, and beckoned Caroline to follow him. He went to a kiosk selling Clippers gear and asked the attendant, a pimply high school kid, for one of the replica sticks. It cost a buck fifty, nearly as much as the two game tickets themselves. He reached in his pocket, slapped down two dollars, and collected two quarters and the stick. It was a pretty cheap stick, but it was emblazoned with the snappy Clippers logo: a grizzled sea captain, fully bearded and in fisherman's togs with requisite cap and buttoned woolen jacket, on skates with a stick in his hand, bursting through an anchor and rope.

Mr. Panski may as well have handed his daughter King Tut's golden mask for the look on Caroline's face. She ran her fingers over the varnished wood, lingering over the slight curve at the widened bottom. She put it on the ground and let it slide across the tiled floor. Then she wound back, taking a few practice swings, threatening her father's shins in the process. "Thank you, Daddy," she whispered.

He kissed Caroline's head. "Our little secret, okay?" he said, winking at her.

She nodded. "Wait. How can I hide this?"

"Who said anything about hiding? You can show it to your mother. But we say it was a giveaway, part of a promotion. She's liable to kill me if you tell her I paid for it. Now, I don't like lying to your mother, but sometimes—"

"I understand."

Why couldn't these stupid boys at the pond be like her dad, or that player from the Clippers? Why did they have to be so rotten? Why did they have to remind her of Carlin's, of the place now too painful to return to without her dad?

When she got back home, her mom was there to meet her, and she was angry. "Where were you?"

"I had to return a school book to Alma."

Mrs. Panski scrutinized her daughter. "Why do you have your skates and stick with you?"

Caroline paused. She could feel the blood rushing to her cheeks. Lying was not something that came easily. "Alma wanted to see them. She's thinking of taking up skating so she can play with me."

"You were supposed to be helping your brother."

"He can help himself."

"Caroline! I asked for your help. I expect to receive it."

"Yes, ma'am," Caroline muttered.

"What's the matter with you? You look like someone's stolen your heart."

Caroline considered telling her mother what happened, but thought better of it. She'd have to reveal that she'd already lied and, besides, how would her mother ever understand anyway? There was no one in the world, she figured, who could really understand. Besides her dad, that is. But he was on the other side of the world.

She felt a burn coming to her eyes and throat, but she managed to swallow it all back. "Nothing's wrong," she whispered.

Caroline trudged up the stairs, heavy-footed. She closed herself in her room, taking the photograph of her father, plopping herself down on her bed, and cradling it to her chest. Small tears leaked from her eyes and trailed down into her hair. It wasn't so long ago that he sat just here, at the very end of her bed, his hands tight, his fingers interlocked and held between his knees, as he tried his best to explain to her why he was heading off to war.

She could tell he was having trouble. The way he kept stopping his sentences, starting them over and over again, searching for the perfect words to say, to fully explain.

"There are communists, you see, and they—"

"What are communists?"

"Communists are really bad people. They don't believe in God, you see, and . . ."

"But you told me you don't believe in God."

"Well, now, that's not exactly what I said. What I said was that I don't believe in organized religion, which isn't the same thing. And in any case, you know your mother doesn't like it when we talk about that, and so, anyway . . . what were we talking about?"

"Communists."

"Yes, communists. You see, they starve their own people. They don't believe in freedom or democracy. They're bad people. And we're locked in a fight with them over who is going to control the world. Well, no, that's not it. You see, they want to control the world. We want to make it safe for freedom. For democracy. So that everyone around the world can have the same opportunities that you have here. In communist countries, well, people don't get to do what they want to do. Do you understand that?"

"I guess I do. You mean like I want to play hockey, but kids in communist countries don't get to."

"Well, it's sort of like that. I mean, you can skate, hit around some pucks, sure. But when you get older, it's time to put that silly stuff aside, become some fine fellow's wife and then become some lucky kid's mother. Everything frivolous comes to an end."

"What's that mean?"

"It means you'll understand it better when you're a bit older."

"I hate when you and Mama say that."

Her father smiled, tousled her hair, and continued. "Part of what it means to be an American is that sometimes you have to sacrifice for other people. People less fortunate. So, you see, sometimes men like me have to go to faraway places to help make the world safer not only for children there but for those just like you, here at home."

"Genevieve's father isn't going to the war because he has children. She said that married men with children don't have to go to the war."

"Well, that's true. But you see, if I go and serve, it'll be good for our family. It'll provide some stability. I don't know if I'll always have the job I have now or even if the plant will always be there. But I'll always have a place in the American military. It's not going anywhere."

Caroline frowned. "Yeah, but you're going somewhere."

"It'll be okay, sweetheart. I promise. I'll go for one year, maybe even less if the war ends before then. It'll go quicker than you think. And then I'll be back home."

"And we'll have a parade?"

"Maybe. Maybe we'll have a parade. But you know what?"

"What?"

"I don't need a parade. Do you know what I need?"

"No."

"Just this."

He reached down as if he was about to hug her, and so Caroline lifted her arms. But he stuck his pointed fingers in her armpits instead and tickled her until she couldn't breathe and begged him to stop, even though she was laughing and smiling. He always knew how to make her laugh. And how to make her smile.

The photograph of her dad slipped from Caroline's fingers. And there it rested, against her side, as she nodded off into an exhausted sleep. But just as quickly, she snapped her head back up, determined to stay awake. She knew that thinking too much about her father just before she went to sleep was a bad idea, that it often induced the dreams. Sometimes they weren't full dreams with beginnings, middles, and ends. Rather they were just flashes, images here and there, products of an over-heated imagination. Other times, the dreams were cobbled together from snatches of radio reports she'd heard and from her father's letters to her mom.

Caroline and Sam received their own letters about once a month, but they were full of questions about what they were doing, how school was going, were they keeping up with their studies, what new things were happening in Baltimore. Caroline dutifully wrote back and answered these questions, but she also asked a bunch of questions of her own. She wanted to know what life was really like over there. But he never seemed to answer, except to say that the soldiers didn't do much, just sat around mostly, talking to one another and trying to stay warm. Caroline suspected that maybe he wrote about these things in the letters to her mother, and maybe this was why Caroline was not allowed to read them.

One time she found one of the letters and read as much of it as she could before she heard her mom coming and had to throw it back on the dresser in her mother's bedroom, where she knew she shouldn't have been snooping in the first place. She managed to read:

I spend a lot of time in my foxhole, just scanning the horizon, waiting for the enemy. But honestly the biggest enemy is boredom. You can only get so much mileage out of those crazy signs the Chinese army left behind before we routed them out. Here are some examples (for your reading pleasure):

"Wait no longer. Hasten to take active measure for peace," "Frontline friendship party was to bring about the positive action for peace," "Think that you don't strive for peace will result in death!"

Isn't that bizarre, Eloise? Really, nothing happens (which I suppose is a good thing). Though the C.O.s are always warning us—"Can happen any minute," they say. "Chinese have fighter jets," they remind us. The younger guys say, "Bring it on." Out of earshot, of course.

I've written to you about Lundeberg and Wysocki, yes? They're my closest mates. Lundeberg is the sweetest guy. Would give you the shirt off his back. One thing, though, kind of drives me nuts. He repeats himself. Man, does he repeat himself. Probably ten times he's told me about his basic training in Baltimore. All about Camp Holabird and Tank Hill. Tells me again how much he loved the Bay and seeing the views over the hills toward Canton and into the Patapsco.

You know this, my dear, even with weak binoculars, you can see every brick on Fort McHenry. It is true, Eloise, it is a beautiful place. And I miss it. When Lundeberg gets to talking about it, I do have to admit it. I smile, tell him, indeed, Baltimore is the "Land of Pleasant Living."

But sometimes, well, I'll admit this, too. Sometimes it just hurts far too much to hear. You know? Gets me thinking of the day I left. Of course I don't have the heart to tell him to shut his mouth. Funny, all Lundeberg's yapping is quite the contrast to the new kid, just shipped in from New Mexico. Name's Tyler. Seems a nice kid. I'll show him the ropes—

She didn't understand the bits about the Chinese; they were fighting in Korea, weren't they? It was all very confusing. She wanted to read more, but the next time she tried to find the letter, it was gone.

Her heart ached to hear that he hurt too much when he thought of home, and she wondered if maybe she should stop writing him letters, to help him not think so much of home. But that would give her a deep hurt to not to do that. A different kind of hurt than

the one she carried around every day, missing
him. She remembered him once telling her
about different kinds of pain, the pain of
thinking too much, how it injured you, and in
different ways at different times. The way you
sometimes rub a cut or bruise, the way the pain
makes you feel alive, the way you can mark the
healing by the degree of pain—perhaps a little
less each time . . .

He didn't need to write anything else about
the day he left for war, how painful that was.
Caroline could remember that for herself
easily enough.

She had wept openly that day at the port
when he left, wrapping herself around him
and leaving a big wet spot on his uniform.
Up to that point, it was the sharpest pain she
had ever imagined. Only now did she think
how difficult that day must have been for him.
Yes, it was horrible for her, watching him walk
away, the person she loved most in the world.
But he had to leave the three people he loved
most. She couldn't even imagine it.

She remembered he'd kissed the top of her head, and she'd heard him swallowing his tears. She knew what that burn felt like, the way it worked its way all the way to your toes. But he was an army man, so crying was not an option. Besides, he wasn't the only one. There were other men, too, just like him, saying goodbye to wives and kids, each of them choking it all back.

He hadn't turned around once he'd started toward the ship. No way he'd have been able to withstand it if he did, Caroline was sure. He'd said his goodbyes and that had to be it. She knew, though, that he was torn apart, and she knew that it was made so much worse by the fact that the brief time he'd had with his family, just four days between basic training in North Carolina and heading off to Korea, had been almost entirely destroyed by a family illness, some kind of nasty flu.

No doubt he'd envisioned family picnics—huge spreads after what Caroline's mom described as the bland fare of the Army camps—out in Patterson Park near the

Chinese Pagoda or in Druid Hill Park while couples rowed their boats in the lake below. Or maybe he'd hoped to picnic on Federal Hill, overlooking the harbor and the wharves.

But that darned virus with its fever, coughs, and aches had been working its way through the entire family for days. Only Sam—the first one to get it—had recovered by the time Caroline's father had to deploy. Caroline and her mom were well enough to see him off by then, but they had both spent almost the entire time he was home in bed.

So he'd spent those precious days doing repairs around the house—he fixed a cracked window, replaced some roof tiles, ripped out and replaced some rotted wood near the flashings. And then, just like that, it was time to go.

All of that was too painful to think about for too long.

Caroline went downstairs, got a glass of water and made herself stay awake. She had her memories and the radio and that one letter all floating around in her head, and that was enough. Sometimes she didn't need any of those things. Often her dreams came almost exclusively from the newsreels she'd seen in school and the ones shown before movies on those rare occasions when she went to the theater with her friends. She hated them, hated the way the announcer's voice was so serious but somehow always managed a slightly upbeat tone, explaining how our brave American soldiers were fighting and winning the war for freedom and democracy. She hated how the reels showed happy smiling men standing in circles smoking and laughing or at tables in mess halls over steaming trays of food. She knew it wasn't like that, at least where her dad was. She knew it was cold and lonely (and dangerous—he wrote of "fighter jets") where he was.

She went back to her room and tried to stay awake for a while longer. But she kept nodding off, in and out of sleep, imagining her father, imagining the world he was seeing. She envisioned him there, in his foxhole, dingy and dirty, but at least out of the freezing wind.

She imagined him staring at the landscape she saw in those newsreels: great open plains pockmarked by stacks of vegetation, the old ripples of abandoned crops still visible. Hills rising from the distant horizon. She envisioned the soldiers taking turns manning their positions along the ridge, guarding against a sneak attack. It was cold. The men dressed in heavy jackets, plumes of breath coming from their mouths and noses, as they tried to warm themselves with cigarettes, conversation, and thoughts of home. As hard as they tried to keep their thoughts from floating home to their loved ones, it must have been impossible.

Caroline knew it hurt her dad to think about home, but she guessed that at times he just couldn't help himself, just like she couldn't help herself from thinking about him. Maybe it was one of those weird good sort of pain things. Or not. She just couldn't know for sure. All she had was her imagination, and that, sometimes, was her worst enemy.

Of course, that kind of pain, even when it got bad, was in some ways a good thing, she knew. Because the alternative was worse. She imagined her dad seeing lines of men, the enemy, coming toward him, coming in for an attack. That, of course, wouldn't be boring, but it certainly would be worse than anything.

Again, she tried to beat away the thoughts of her dad. Better to think about something else. Negroes in school with white kids? That was something new. And how to feel about that. As she told her friends, it didn't bother her any. But of course that was easy to say about something you hadn't actually experienced.

Oh, well—who knew if it would ever actually come to be? If it did, she'd deal with it then. For now, she needed to get some sleep.

3

THE MIDDLE OF THE NIGHT. The world was very, very still.

Beautiful lay curled up at the foot of the bed. Caroline's eyes were wide open, and she breathed heavily, pulled out of sleep by another one of those nasty dreams. She needed to shake the dream from her head. So she slowly got out of bed, driven by something deep and unresolved. The dog stirred, but didn't wake.

Caroline moved more quickly now, her actions practiced. She quietly slipped on layers of clothes, casting shadows across her room. She plucked her stick and skates off the floor and made her way to her door. She opened it, peeked out, and then slowly closed the door behind her. She tiptoed her way through the hall, down the stairs, and through the front door—a slow, tortuous process, but one she managed to accomplish without a sound.

Along the street, she kept her head down. It was a route she knew well, so she could keep her eyes mainly on the sidewalk, as if looking up would invite trouble, allowing any number of threats into her visual field. She kept going until she reached the pond.

In the moonlight, the pond was a magical place. Piles of garbage had been transformed into strange and shimmering shapes. The pond surface was a mess of blade scratches and nicks, but even this had a magical, artistic quality, resembling a print of a painting her mother had recently picked up by an artist named Jackson Pollock.

Caroline inhaled. She put on her skates, grabbed her stick, and shot out onto the ice. Soon, she was tearing up the entire pond, showing off some deft stick handling. She pumped her legs and sped from one end of the ice to the other, the stick across her knees, and then wound up for some high octane slap shots, before coming to a quick stop in a spray of ice.

Then, in the very near distance, came the sound of exploding glass. She stopped and listened, alert and on edge, like a skittish deer.

The source of the sound revealed itself: a drunken man tottering on the sidewalk, not far from the edge of the lot. Initially, he presented no threat—he stood a good distance away. But Caroline was wary. She looked around and, for the first time, realized the compromised position she'd placed herself in.

Suddenly, the area appeared menacing. She could see that the man had noticed her, standing silently and looking in her direction. Just staring at her. A halo of light and vaporous exhalations surrounded him, giving him a spectral glow.

Caroline took off.

She tore across the ice to the other end, where she grabbed her shoes and continued her flight on land. She was on skates and carrying her stick, so this was awkward business. Across the lot, through the alley, onto the street, and *crash!* Caroline toppled over and spilled onto the sidewalk.

Breathing heavily, she tugged at her skates until she managed to get them off and then resumed her run. A sock fell from one of the skates as she went, and it wasn't long before she was limping badly, hobbling down the deserted city street in the middle of the night.

Caroline was in tears by the time she limped up the steps toward her front door. Then the door swung open to reveal her mother, standing in the doorway in her bathrobe. She was furious.

The rage sputtered from Mrs. Panski in seething, half-formed words as she navigated a dizzying line between screaming and whispering so as not to wake Sam. The result was a strange mixture of sounds squirming through her clenched teeth as she steered her daughter up the stairs and into her bedroom.

"Sit!" Mrs. Panski commanded, pointing to the edge of Caroline's bed. Caroline landed there and waited. One foot was bare, and her ankle was badly swollen. Mrs. Panski came in holding an ice pack. She slapped it down onto the ankle.

"Ouch! That hurts!"

"Good." The fury hadn't yet subsided, and Mrs. Panski's face was a deep red. As she worked her daughter's ankle, not at all gently, little wisps of hair kept escaping the band tying it back, giving her the appearance of a madwoman in half-light working some strange machinery. "What were you thinking?"

"I want to play hockey."

"It's the middle of the night! Do you have any idea what could have happened to you?"

"Nothing happened."

"No? What do you call this?" Mrs. Panski dug an unsympathetic finger into Caroline's ankle.

"Ow!"

"By the grace of God it was nothing worse. Look me in the eye and promise you will never do something like that again."

"I promise."

"Look me in the eye."

Caroline did so. "I promise."

Mrs. Panski wrapped Caroline's ankle with gauze and tape as if she was an expert in treating such injuries. Caroline didn't ask how she knew. She figured it was simply something that resided in the toolbox of every woman's maternal skills. Finally, Mrs. Panski got up, paused, and then announced, "I'm taking away your skates."

"But, Mom!"

"This is not a debate."

"But it's not fair. Why can't I play hockey?"

"Girls don't play hockey."

"That's what the boys say."

"They're right."

"But—"

"Not another word. You have school in the morning."

Mrs. Panski turned out the light and retreated toward her bedroom door where a dim hall light framed her. Caroline watched as her mother pitched slightly from side to side.

That was another thing she didn't ask her mother about, how she'd got that limp. Well, she did ask about it once, years earlier, and her mother replied, "I was born with it. Now go clean yourself up for supper." Caroline knew not to ask again.

CAROLINE STRETCHED, threw back her covers, and hopped out of bed. As soon as her feet hit the floor, she let out a cry of pain and fell back onto the bed. She looked down at a blue and purple ankle swollen to twice its normal size. Somehow, she'd forgotten.

She managed to get dressed and then limped down the stairs and into the kitchen where her mother was busy over the stove. Sam was already at the table, chomping his bacon. Mrs. Panski turned and her eyes widened when she saw Caroline standing there with her foot hovering above the ground. "Look at you!" she exclaimed.

"It really hurts."

"Of course it does. Sit."

Caroline took her place at the table as Mrs. Panksi wrapped ice in a wet towel and put it on Caroline's ankle.

"How are you planning to walk to school?"

"I can manage."

Mrs. Panski placed a plate in front of her daughter. "Eat."

Caroline obeyed.

Sam eyed his sister, an impish smile spreading across his face. It was obvious that Caroline was in trouble, a prospect Sam clearly found irresistibly wonderful. "What did you do?" he asked.

Mrs. Panski took Sam's empty plate. "Your sister decided to run off to that frozen pond and play hockey and she hurt her ankle." The plate banged against the side of the sink, producing a sharp piercing sound. "I hope it knocked some sense into her, too."

Sam made a face. He wasn't about to let this go so easily. "The boys make fun of me 'cause of her," he said. "Whoever heard of a girl playing hockey?"

But Sam did not get the reaction he obviously wanted. Instead, and in addition to Caroline's evil eye, Mrs. Panski shot one of her own at him. "Go get washed up for school," she ordered.

Sam ran out, but not before sticking his tongue out at Caroline.

Caroline finished her breakfast and, wincing with each step, hobbled over to the sink with her plate.

Mrs. Panski sighed and grabbed the plate from her daughter. "Stay here. I've got something."

From the top of the stairs, Caroline watched her mother rooting around in the basement until she pulled out two crutches from behind some boxes.

"Try these," she said, handing the crutches to Caroline when she returned to the kitchen.

Caroline placed the crutches under each arm and frowned. The metal ends dug into her armpits. She shifted them around, but to no avail.

"This is worse than just walking on my foot," she said, leaning the crutches back toward her mother.

But the moment she put pressure on her foot, she gasped at the pain.

"Take them. You need them," Mrs. Panski said.

"But they hurt."

"It's one hurt or the other. And there's no way your ankle will heal unless you stay off it."

"But it's really uncomfortable."

What Caroline really wanted was to stay home from school and sit with her foot propped up. That would help it heal, she was sure. But one glance at her mother—who stared at her with hands on her hips as if waiting for the chance to say *No, don't even ask if you can stay home*—and she decided not to bother. Besides, the prospect of her mother glowering at her all day was worse than making her way to school on the stupid crutches.

So Caroline hobbled awkwardly down the front steps—one foot, land, the other foot, held aloft, three times until she reached the bottom—to where Alma stood watching on the sidewalk, mouth hanging open in shock.

"What happened to you?"

"Take my books," Caroline said, handing them over and steadying herself. Already, the hollows under her arms ached from the pressure of the crutches. Her coat helped, but not that much.

Alma's look told Caroline there was no way she could escape telling the whole gruesome story. So she obliged, leaving nothing out, and even embellishing the part with the drunk guy. "I guess I just got kind of spooked," she wrapped up as she and Alma made their way toward school.

"That's a crazy thing you did, Caroline Panksi. Don't you know any better?"

"I guess I don't."

"Why do you want to play hockey so bad anyway?"

"I don't know. It's fun."

"There are other ways to have fun."

"It's more like—when I'm out there it's as if all of Baltimore, all of the world, is just gone. It's hard to explain."

"But if you can skate so good, why don't you just, you know, skate? Like girls do. I can't imagine any man wanting to marry a hockey player. What if you lost your two front teeth?"

"I don't care about marrying any man."

"But, Caroline, that's why God put us on this earth. I can't wait to get married, and have eleven children—six boys and five girls—and have my own house, with a washing machine and a television, and a vacuum cleaner and a television—"

"You said that already."

"Well then, we'll have two. Or even one for every room in the house."

"That's ridiculous."

Suddenly Alma stopped. She looked up and pointed. "Hey, look at that. Something's going on at the high school."

A large group of people milled about excitedly on the sidewalk. It was a larger crowd than the day before. As Caroline and Alma got closer, they watched two police cars pull up. Officers got out of each and went around to open up the back doors, where four black students got out—two girls in one car, two boys in another. The officers escorted the students toward the school.

The black students looked dignified and calm—the girls both wore bright colored sweaters buttoned at the very top of their neckline and radiating frills of lace, while the boys wore blazers and dark trousers. But Caroline sensed a palpable nervousness, even fear, simmering just below the surface. No one in the crowd shouted or waved signs, but there was definitely tension in the air. Caroline felt like it was a face off. As if one false move from someone in the crowd could unleash something really bad.

She tugged on Alma's sweater. "Let's get out of here."

5

"WE GIVE THANKS FOR these our gifts which we are about to receive through the grace of our Lord. Father, son, holy spirit. Amen."

The Panskis dug in, though Caroline stared at her plate and ate slowly. After a while, she looked up. "Mama?"

"Hmm?"

"We saw some Negroes at the high school today."

Mrs. Panski nodded. "I heard about that on the radio. Integrating the schools."

"What's integrating?"

"It means they're allowing Negroes to go to school with whites."

Sam snorted and shook his head. "I don't want no darkies at my school."

Both Caroline and Mrs. Panski said in unison, "Shut your mouth, Sam."

"Those people just want an education like everyone else," Mrs. Panski chided. "These are special students in any case. Real smart. They're attending the white high schools that offer the 'A' courses. For the best students."

"Will there be integration at my school, too?"

"That I don't know. Eat up now."

"Mama?" Caroline asked again.

"Hmm?"

"Where'd you get the crutches from?"

Mrs. Panski stopped chewing, considered, then swallowed her food very deliberately. She stole a glance at Sam.

"Eat your supper, you two."

They ate in silence, and Caroline sensed it wasn't the best idea to keep asking for an answer her mother clearly didn't want to give. So she let it drop. But that evening, after supper, Mrs. Panski pulled Caroline into her bedroom.

"Come in here. I want to show you something," she said.

Caroline hoped it was going to be her skates, that her mother had reconsidered and was going to give them back to her. She could see them on the floor next to the closet, in their deplorable condition; it was so easy to notice now: the stitching threatening to burst along the seams, the blades no sharper than a butter knife.

But Mrs. Panski made no mention of the skates. Instead, she sighed and walked over to her dresser where there rested a picture of herself in a wedding dress with her new husband standing next to her holding her hand. Next to that was the picture of him in his army uniform, the same photograph Caroline had in her room.

Mrs. Panski opened a drawer in her bureau and pulled out a small brocaded box. She opened it and took out another photograph—a group of hockey players, in uniform, standing square and smiling, an unintimidating bunch, to be sure. But that was something people would notice only secondarily. The first thing they'd see, what was plain as day, was that all the players were women. And, there, in the middle of the second row stood Caroline's mother, also smiling, looking very beautiful, and wearing goalie gear.

She handed it to Caroline, who studied it wide-eyed.

"This is you?"

"It sure is."

"I don't understand."

Mrs. Panski patted the bed for Caroline to sit. "I'll tell you the whole story."

Caroline took her place on the bed, her attention rapt on her mother.

"It was just a novelty at first. And we were rough, I'll admit that. A bunch of ladies flailing about on the ice taking whacks and more often than not whiffing at the pucks. But Coach taught us the x's and o's and eventually we got the hang of it. The better ones among us quickly floated to the top. We were girls who were hockey players and not just girls on the ice barreling into each other for the amusement of the men who came to watch."

"And you were the goalie?"

"That was by accident, actually. The regular goalie had taken a puck across her calf in practice one evening and I filled in. For some reason, I found it kind of easy." She smiled, remembering. "I turned aside shot after shot. It was more reaction than anything else. I'd just kick out my leg or shoot out my glove and somehow blocked pretty much everything my teammates tossed my way. Soon, shooting practice turned into a game of who could get it past me. I can still picture Coach standing there with his whistle hanging half in and half out of his mouth, the other ladies lined up to cheer me and then each new shooter. One thing was soon pretty clear: I was the new goalie." Mrs. Panski smiled at her daughter. "And I don't mind saying, I was pretty darn good, too."

"I don't doubt that."

"Once I realized I was going to be playing goalie, then it was practice, practice, practice. And that was something I happily took to. At home, I'd take a tennis ball and whiz it against the side of a brick wall, over and over, catching and blocking each rebound. Everyone thought I was a natural. But that wasn't true. It was work. And work was something I wasn't afraid of."

"I don't doubt that, either." Caroline pointed at the picture. "Tell me about your games."

"It started on a cold January evening in 1937. It was the new league's very first game ever. I was the goalie for the Spitfires. We were playing the Glamour Girls, over at the Sports Center. On North and Calvert, just a few blocks from Penn Station. Huge old place, like a cavern. Smelled of sweat and age. Plenty of National Bohemian beer had been swilled and spilled in there."

"Mrs. Eloise Panski, star goalie for the Spitfires," Caroline said, smiling.

"Remember, I was Eloise Weatherbee back then, not Panski. Anyway, I took my place in front of the cage. I must have looked really odd, I'm sure. Lipstick, blush, permed hair set with curlers—that was a team requirement, believe it or not—but all of that was hidden the moment I pulled on that gruesome looking mask. I had the same warm-up routine: slide from side to side, pole to pole, nicking up the ice in front of me. I took it very seriously. But even then, I knew, we were out there mostly just to sell tickets and beer. For that first game, there was a reporter there for the Sun papers. My old coach was thrilled with that. I can still remember their exchange: 'Coach, what is the appeal of these ladies on the ice? Most people prefer to see their girls performing axels and butterfly jumps.'

"Coach gave that sly grin of his. He spoke loudly, so that everyone taking their seats could hear. He was a natural promoter; the man may have been a carnival barker in a previous life. 'True, they play hell for leather hockey,' he said, 'And put all their hearts into it. They take their wallops and bruises, but when a girl takes a bad tumble, she picks herself right up and grins. But instead of rubbing her bruise, she straightens her hair.'

"Everybody laughed. It was a spectacle. But like I said, I took it very seriously. We all did. Sure, it wasn't the National Hockey League, but we didn't go easy on each other. The girls had no fear of going into the corner to dig out pucks. And when the puck dropped to start a game, honestly, the place went wild. It didn't matter which team scored. The people went crazy for every goal. There was no home team. During the intermissions, about a dozen boys would jump out on the ice. Each of them carried a snow shovel. Then, side by side, they would put their shovels on the ice and make their way across the rink, smoothing the surface."

"Tell me about your first game."

"It was a special night. For one thing, during an intermission, when I skated to the bench for some water, I noticed a really handsome guy in the crowd. He smiled at me. Even with that hockey mask, I guess he thought I was pretty."

"You're talking about Daddy?"

"Let me finish. First, there was the game. We were up by one goal. One of the Glamour Girls skated toward me, barely five seconds left on the clock."

Mrs. Panski got up, then crouched into position, mimicking a goalie's readied stance.

"The crowd was on their feet, breathless. 5-4-3-2 … The Glamour Girl let fly an absolute screamer that I snared out of the air as time expired."

Mrs. Panski closed her fist onto an imaginary puck as Caroline beamed up at her.

"After the game, I was the last one out. Often no one waited for me—it was an eternity taking off all that equipment and they all had to get back home to make supper. But when I came out of the locker room and stepped into that dank hallway, I heard someone. 'I didn't think you'd ever come out,' he said. I jumped, and I saw a man step toward me. I was startled, but he was smiling, and he seemed kind. And then I recognized him as the handsome man I'd exchanged looks with during intermission."

"Daddy?"

"He said, 'You wanna get out of here?'"

"That was how you met him? At a hockey game?" Caroline smiled, big and wide, thrilled with every detail of the story.

"We strolled around the Washington Monument at Mount Vernon Place. I can still picture the way the cobblestone was glistening in the lamplight. And he was so sweet. Said to me, 'I don't know how someone so athletic can also look like a movie star.' I reminded him about Sonja Henie. He just smiled at me and leaned in for a kiss."

Mrs. Panski smiled at the memory and put her fingers to her lips, as if she could still feel the sensation, even after so many years.

"Maaamaaaa—" Caroline groaned, but she didn't really mind hearing about the kiss. In fact, she loved hearing about her parents being in love.

"So that was hockey, how it started. How I became Mrs. Eloise Panski. But not too long after, well, I was pretty enormous when I was pregnant with you. Final few weeks of the pregnancy, I barely walked anymore. Waddled was more like it, always threatening to tip over. But I kept up my chores—preparing meals, washing and ironing clothes, sweeping the feather duster along the porcelains, rubbing oils into the dark furniture.

When Daddy returned from work at Bethlehem Steel, he'd place his pail on the table, give me a kiss, and take off his dirty clothing. I'd take the pail to the kitchen for cleaning and carry the clothes to the cellar to dunk them in sudsy water, scrubbing that stubborn residue with that coarse brush we have, and hang them along the line in the back of the house so that they'd be dry for next morning. The same routine—every day, until you arrived. Sweet Caroline."

Mrs. Panski rubbed her hand gently along Caroline's forehead.

"And then the routine resumed once again. It was a happy time. Some women might have seen all the housework and a new baby as stifling—no room for anything creative. No room even for yourself. But for me, it was a thrill. I had a home, a husband I loved, and I had a beautiful new baby girl. It was hard to imagine anything better. I hardly had a moment to even think about hockey."

Caroline looked again at the photograph, at her smiling and radiant mother. "You're so pretty."

Mrs. Panski took the photograph from her daughter and returned it to the box in the bureau. "Don't sound so surprised."

"I'm not surprised. I know you're pretty. It's just that ... I don't understand."

"There's lots you don't understand."

"Why didn't you ever tell me before?"

"And encouraged you even more? Last thing you needed."

"But if you loved it so much and had so much fun, why are you so against me playing hockey, and why are you telling me all this now?"

"So you can see that I'm not just trying to make you unhappy. I understand your desire to play. I do. But you need to listen to me. It's true what they say. Hockey is for boys. You want to figure skate, fine. But there's nothing but trouble in hockey."

Caroline thought for a long moment. "Your leg?" she finally asked.

Mrs. Panski nodded.

"You told me you were born with that limp."

"I'm sorry I lied to you."

"Is that the real reason you stopped playing?"

"I told you, I met your father."

"He made you stop playing?"

"And I became pregnant. Weren't you listening?"

"I made you stop playing?"

"I became what I was supposed to become—a wife, a mother, a homemaker. Girls can have all the dreams and games they want. But someday, girls turn into women. And then it's time to put all that silly stuff aside."

"But you got to play. You just told me—"

"I didn't know any better. And neither did my parents. They were too busy working all the time. You have the benefit of having a mother who knows better. Dreams are for girls, not women.

"But I'm still a girl."

"And one day, sooner than you think, you'll be a woman."

"But, mama—"

"No buts. Now get washed up for bed."

Caroline didn't move.

"Go."

After Caroline disappeared down the hall, Mrs. Panski drew the picture back out of the box. The young woman in the goalie gear and the big smile looked back at her. Mrs. Panski looked out the window and then returned the photo to the box, stood, and turned out the light.

6

LIKE THE REST of her classmates, Caroline sat at her desk wondering what was going on out in the hall. A couple of kids near the doorway strained to hear what Miss Bloom and their solemn-looking principal, Mr. Podolski, were talking about. Whatever it was, it looked serious. After a few moments, Miss Bloom entered the classroom, and everyone straightened up and stopped their murmuring.

"Children, your attention, please. We have a new student joining us today."

"Boy or girl?" one of the boys asked.

"A young man."

Alma looked at Caroline and made a face.

The door opened again, and everyone turned as the principal steered a scared looking

Negro boy into the room. Miss Bloom cocked her chin toward an empty seat in the middle row, right next to Caroline's. "Joseph, take a seat there in the second row."

Joseph tentatively walked to his new desk, his chin buried in his chest and his eyes on the ground. The rest of the students murmured and looked to their neighbors, unsure how to compute this unprecedented turn of events.

Beatrice raised her hand. "Miss Bloom?"

"What is it, Beatrice?"

"Isn't it illegal to have Negroes in schools with whites?"

"Apparently, it isn't. Now, everyone please open your math textbooks—"

"Miss Bloom?" Beatrice spoke up again.

"What is it now?"

"I thought it was illegal—"

"Joseph has just moved to Baltimore from the south, and his Daddy ... well, there are special circumstances ... and I do not need to explain this to you. We have work to do. Now, open your mathematics textbooks to Chapter 14."

A few of the students still sat frozen, while others looked warily at the new arrival who, quite conspicuously, did not have a book.

"Do I need to repeat myself?" Miss Bloom boomed.

The students hopped to, but the nervous energy did not fully dissipate even as Miss Bloom began chalking up the board with some rudimentary algebra.

Joseph looked around, obviously nervous. One girl in the front row turned and openly scowled at him. He continued looking around the room until he caught eyes with Caroline, who managed to give him a shy smile. After a few moments, she scooted her desk toward him and laid out her book between them.

Miss Bloom watched but said nothing. The students in the class murmured to each other as Miss Bloom turned back to the board.

"Thank you," Joseph whispered.

Miss Bloom clapped a stick against the board and the students got the message. They began their lessons with renewed focus.

During lunch, Joseph sat by himself in the cafeteria, a long table's only occupant, nibbling on a paltry lunch. Caroline looked over at him, something her friends noticed, but she did not join him.

Three white boys did, however, including Alan, Caroline's nemesis from the hockey pond. Alan "accidentally" spilled some milk on Joseph and then walked away laughing. Joseph didn't react, as if this was all a normal part of the school day. Caroline continued to watch, but she didn't get up to help. In fact, no one did, not even the teachers. But even if she had wanted to help him, he was already up and heading out. To the bathroom, she guessed, so he could get cleaned up.

When the bell rang signaling the end of the school day, the students poured out through the doors—yelling boys, laughing girls, making their way down the front steps of the school. It had been a couple of days since she stopped using the crutches, but Caroline still walked with a limp so Alma, Beatrice, and Genevieve walked slowly so she could keep up.

"What's eating you?" Alma turned to ask Caroline as she fell behind again. "Cat got your tongue?"

"I'm just thinking it must be hard for that boy. New school, being the only colored boy. I can't imagine. Seems nice enough to me."

"Sounds like you've got a little crush."

"Don't be ridiculous. I certainly do not."

"I don't even think that's legal in Maryland," Beatrice chimed in. "Really, Caroline. It's all good and well that you like our new colored friend, but everyone saw the way you looked at him in class."

Caroline's face reddened. "I don't know what you're talking about."

"He's colored, Caroline," Beatrice said. "He might very well be a nice boy. But he's a colored boy, and there's nothing but trouble in that."

Genevieve glared at her friend. "Oh, shush, Beatrice."

"I'm just saying you should keep your distance is all."

The girls reached their separation point and said goodbye to one another.

"See you," Genevieve said. "And Caroline? Don't pay Bee any mind."

"I'm just saying is all," Beatrice said before she and Genevieve headed in one direction, Caroline and Alma in the other.

The girls walked silently. Alma looked at her friend. "You have been quiet, Caroline."

Caroline swallowed. She had been thinking of Joseph, but she knew she couldn't admit that out loud. There was something about him— she didn't know what. She had wanted to talk to him at lunch, but something like that just wasn't done, and no one, not even her friends, would understand.

But that was just the point, wasn't it? What if she believed that Joseph could be the only one who might understand her? When she looked at him, she saw the same thing in his eyes that she saw in her own while staring at herself in the mirror as she combed and curled her hair each morning. It was a certain kind of fear, a trepidation, a belief that something terrible was on the way, that life will throw not its blessings but its banes at you, and that it could happen any day at any time. Her father was fighting in a war and she knew what that meant, what it could mean. And the way Joseph had about him, like he too was holding on to something sad, something way beyond him, deep inside.

Of course, she couldn't say these things to Alma. Alma was fun and being around her rarely failed to make Caroline happy. But she just couldn't understand how Caroline felt, not with her own daddy at home with her. So Caroline didn't bother to try to explain.

Caroline walked as if she were dragging a weight behind her, a weight from the whole wide world that pressed down on her. It wasn't just Alma. No one understood her—not her mother, not her brother, not her friends. Not really, anyway. Only one person, and he was so far away. She struggled against the weight of it all, consciously straightening her shoulders with every other step, the universe pushing them back into a hunched shape as she moved, a push and pull that seemed unrelenting.

But then she entered the house and there, awaiting her arrival, sitting by the front door, was a new pair of skates. She rushed to them and picked them up, running a finger softly and carefully across the very tip of the blades.

"Those are for figure skating," Mrs. Panski said from the kitchen doorway.

Caroline ran to her, throwing her arms around her mother's aproned waist. "Thank you, Mama. They're beautiful."

"I got them secondhand, from Mr. Reider's. They were inexpensive, but they'll do. Certainly better than those old ones you had."

"They're beautiful, Mama. I love them."

Mrs. Panski crossed her arms and furrowed her brows at Caroline.

"Promise me you'll be careful."

"I promise."

"Caroline—"

"I promise."

"No more of this running off in the middle of the night."

"No, Mama. Only in the day."

7

THE NOISE COMING from the kitchen sounded like a goose.

When they first heard it, they all looked up. Sam, Caroline, and their mother had all been in the front room, each lost in a book: *Belles on Their Toes* for Caroline; *A Town Like Alice* for Mrs. Panski, and a *Plastic Man* comic book for Sam. Caroline got up and went to the kitchen only to find Beautiful standing there, tail wagging, and water dribbling from her muzzle into little splashes on the floor. She looked like she was smiling.

Caroline bent down to scratch the dog's head. "Was that you making that noise, my beautiful little Beautiful?"

The dog's tail whirled and helicoptered.

"You swallow a goose?"

Beautiful stood on her hind legs, her front paws scratching into Caroline's shins. Beautiful's nails never did any more damage than leaving small white lines on Caroline's skin and the scratches felt good somehow, an affirmation of life from the little doggy who loved her so much.

She picked up Beautiful and nuzzled her, carrying her into the front room. "I think it was her," Caroline said.

"What kind of noise was that?" Mrs. Panski asked the dog. "Can you do it again?"

But Beautiful did nothing other than squirm out of Caroline's arms and drop to the ground, where she pranced over to her favorite spot on the rug next to the big red chair Mrs. Panski favored. Beautiful circled the rug three times before plopping to the ground in a tight ball. The family watched her, smiling as they often did at Beautiful's antics.

Later, with everyone spread out in various parts of the house, Beautiful made the noise again. Caroline was in her room, daydreaming, but slowly the realization that the noise was back dawned on her. She got up and went downstairs to see Beautiful still curled up near the chair.

"You okay, girl?" she asked.

The dog blinked at her a few times and within moments fell back asleep, leaking little whistling noises as she snored.

At first Caroline was worried, but soon she forgot about the noise. Instead of worrying about strange noises or her father in danger far away, she buttoned up her coat, slung her new skates over her shoulder and headed for the pond.

As usual, Caroline arrived to see there were already a dozen or so boys playing hockey. They were so into it, in fact, that it took a while for any of them to register that Caroline was standing there at the edge of the pond, her new skates on her feet, a look of steely determination in her eye.

"Look who's here," Alan declared.

"I just came to skate. That's all," she said, remembering her promise to her mother.

"We don't play with girls," one of the boys declared.

"Yeah. We don't play with girls," another chimed in.

Caroline wanted to tell this last kid that he looked like an idiot, standing there with a stupid smile on his face, repeating what his friend already said as if he didn't have an original thought anywhere in his stupid little brain. But she bit her lip. She didn't need any trouble.

"I told you I'm only here to skate." Caroline tiptoed toward the ice. She knew she should have just let it go at that. But as she listened to the dummies laugh and make snide comments, she couldn't help herself. She knew she was going to say something else. The words seemed to spring up from somewhere deep inside, against her will. "But I could beat you if I wanted to," she said, stepping onto the ice.

At that, the boys laughed hysterically. It was the laughing that got her. It was a cackling sort of thing, a hyena-like peal echoing and bouncing off the nearby buildings, slipping across the ice, doubling back on itself, a chorus of idiocy. She wanted to tell them that they sounded like stupid little girls, but she couldn't figure out how to tell them that without insulting little girls. She felt as if some alien force deep inside her was pushing her forward, telling her that the last thing she should do is turn and walk away, go home, let them win.

But simply taking her rightful place on the far end of the ice, practicing her skating, wouldn't do either. Because she knew full well they wouldn't let her be. They'd be watching her, shouting things at her, maybe even skating next to her and knocking her down. They'd make her the focus of their stupid game.

So she skated directly toward one of the boys and yanked the stick out of his hand.

"Hey!" he yelled. He was at least a head shorter than she was. She loomed over him, his stick in her hand, and stared down at him. All he managed to come up with was, "Dumb girl," something even his friends recognized as completely lame.

The boy backed away, muttering about stupid girls and figure skating in an attempt to save face.

Caroline looked at all the other boys gathered around her and banged the stick on the ice. "Well, are we playing or not?"

The boys snorted and shook their heads and then someone dropped the puck and passed it toward Caroline. She took it with ease, skated a bit, eluded some poke checks, and slid it to a boy who fired a shot. He didn't score a goal, but it was a pretty play. A newfound level of respect seemed to ripple through the boys. But they were not all convinced. No way.

As they skated back and forth, Caroline proved she was good, but several times she lost the puck or fired an errant or intercepted pass.

She could play, but she certainly hadn't shown them she was some kind of superstar.

Until, that is, she collected a pass and charged toward the net. Facing down two defenders, she executed a nifty little twirl—shades of figure skating, it appeared—deked between them both, and continued charging toward net, leaving the defenders a tangled mess on the ice. Alan charged behind. He reached out his stick to trip her up, but she remained just a step ahead. She raced toward the goal, wound up, and sizzled a slapshot past the goalie and into the makeshift netting.

Cheers went up across the pond. Arms raised, Caroline circled back toward the midline when Alan rammed into her, sending her sprawling onto the ice. Several of the boys groaned. But Alan stared them down, and no one, it seemed, was willing to challenge him. Nor was anyone willing to help Caroline up. She lay there for a few stunned moments before collecting herself. Then she dropped the stick onto the ice, skated to the edge, and stepped off the pond. Alone. No one even asked if she was okay.

Dusk pooled in the western sky—a dark bank of clouds lending a dismal grayness to an already colorless scene. Through this, Caroline trudged toward home, broken less in body than in spirit. Sore, yes, but that would heal. It wasn't the physical pain that got to her. No, that she could handle. It was the unfairness of a world that made rules without her input and against her will.

The next morning, as the sun broke the horizon, Caroline was sound asleep, a slight smile on her lips and a look on her face that spoke of untroubled dreams. But she suddenly gasped and thrust upward, jolted out of sleep by something unpleasant: a bad dream, a premonition, something deep and unknown. She looked around, blinked, exhaled a few times, and remembered everything. Her father was in Korea. The hockey boys were jerks. Alan was a bully. That poor Joseph had to go to school with no friends. Why was it that sometimes bad dreams and reality were one and the same?

She began a slow crawl out of bed and into full consciousness, then dressed and made her sluggish way to the breakfast table.

Sam shoveled oatmeal into his mouth, the gluttonous noise he made the only sounds during an otherwise silent breakfast. Caroline pushed her oatmeal around with a spoon, occasionally reaching down to give Beautiful a distracted head scratch. The dog reacted to her fingers by thrusting her head up to meet the outstretched digits, but when she stretched too far, it set off a series of chokes and dry heaves and she immediately lowered her head again. Caroline hardly noticed the dog's struggles.

"You okay?" Mrs. Panksi placed her hand on Caroline's forehead. "You don't feel warm."

"Just not hungry is all."

Caroline excused herself and left early for school, choosing to walk alone. A few houses down from hers, two men sat on the stoop in heavy coats and gloves. Caroline waved and they waved back.

As she walked past, she heard one of the men say, "Sweet kid."

"Father's in Korea." the other said.

"Yeah. What a mess …"

Caroline hurried on down the street.

IT WAS STILL A BIT EARLY for the first bell and the school building had an expectant air about it. Caroline milled around out front, thinking briefly of heading over to the frozen pond—for what reason she wasn't sure. Perhaps she could study the smooth surface and glean some advantage for the next time she'd be out there. For there would be a next time, she resolved. But she knew she couldn't get there and back before the first bell.

Then she saw Joseph, the new kid. He looked like he was freezing, teeth chattering and shivering in a jacket far too skimpy for the cold December morning.

"Hi," Caroline said as he approached.

"Hi," Joseph muttered shyly, looking down

at his feet as if Caroline's eyes contained something radioactive.

For a long time, this was all that passed between them. The silence hung heavily, interrupted only by the *whoosh* of a passing truck. It became obvious that Joseph was not going to say anything else. Something more than just shyness defined his presence, defined his whole persona. He would not look at her. But it was different from the way those jerks at the pond wouldn't look at her. Those guys wouldn't look because they didn't think she was worth the effort. But with Joseph, it was different. He clutched his arms around himself, as if he was afraid of taking up too much space. Like he was scared of getting too close, or something. But why should he be scared of a girl, Caroline wondered.

Just standing there, just the two of them, not talking to one another—it was unnerving. Caroline hated it. She hated being ignored.

"Do you always get here so early?" she blurted.

Joseph looked around, took his time in responding, and finally addressed Caroline's shoes. "My granny's crazy. Makes me leave an hour early so I won't be late."

"So where are you coming from anyway?" she asked.

"Over near East Preston way."

"You walk from up there?"

Joseph kicked at the cement. He frowned as if he'd been hoping his last sentence would be the end of it. He looked around and Caroline wondered if he was waiting for someone. But finally he responded, "How else?"

"I dunno," Caroline shrugged. "I live on South Clinton. Highlandtown."

Joseph didn't acknowledge this.

Caroline gave up and turned away, her back to him. Clearly this boy didn't want to talk. She couldn't figure it out. Maybe they were all the same—her brother, the jerks on the pond, now Joseph. None of them would even talk to a girl unless to say something nasty. Only her dad was different. Maybe boys needed to become men before they became human beings. But then Joseph spoke up again, so suddenly Caroline nearly jumped out of her skin.

"They say soon enough all the schools will be integrated. But I don't know why I can't just go to school with people like me. I don't want to be here. No one wants me here."

"That's not true."

He looked straight at her.

"Granny told me back in the day, colored boys couldn't come down this way at all. Toward the park south of Eager was off limits. Get chased out. Now I gotta walk through there all by myself to get to a school where no one wants me."

She straightened her shoulders. "I'm sure there's plenty of people who think it's just fine that you go here."

Caroline knew what it felt like to not be seen, to be dismissed like you weren't worth anything, and she decided right then and there it would be her job to make Joseph feel welcome, to fill him in on the peculiarities of the place she called home, even though she wasn't particularly fond of it herself. There were some good things about the area, she figured. Why else would her grandparents have come here from Europe, processed through Broadway Pier, and then stayed in Baltimore?

"Those days are over," she said. "You don't need to worry about that anymore. For the most part, kids are pretty nice in this school." She wasn't sure she believed that, but she felt it her duty to say it.

"My mama came from Roanoke. Went down to South Carolina and met my daddy. So she doesn't know anything about Baltimore. Just listens to my granny."

"My grandparents came from Europe, you go back far enough. I guess your family comes from Africa?"

"I guess so."

"Well, I'm glad you're here." Caroline held out her hand for Joseph to shake. But he either didn't see it, or ignored it.

"Well, I'm not."

"I'm sure Jackie Robinson didn't want to play baseball with white people, either, but he does all right."

"I don't like baseball."

"Me neither. I like hockey."

Joseph turned in Caroline's direction, but the look on his face and the one he gave her spoke of utter confusion. "Huh?"

Caroline felt the blood in her veins start to boil. Were they really all alike? Every single one of them? "You gonna tell me that a girl can't play hockey, too?"

"I don't know what on earth you're talking about."

"You don't know what hockey is?"

Joseph shook his head.

This kid had never even heard of hockey?

"Fastest game on skates," Caroline said.

"Roller skates?"

"Ice skates."

Joseph looked down again. "I've never seen anyone skate on ice."

"Really? I'll have to show you sometime."

The steps were filling up now as the time for the school day to start drew nearer.

Although one or two students shot nasty looks toward him, Joseph's presence had lost much of its novelty. Most of the kids ignored him, but a few did a double take when they saw him chatting so casually with a white girl right out front on the school steps. But no one said a word until Alma came racing up.

"Where were you? I waited."

"I'm sorry. I woke up late," Caroline said. "I just got here."

"Oh." Alma looked puzzled. "But if you woke up late, how—"

"I just got here," Caroline repeated.

Alma looked at Joseph, who looked at her, then at Caroline, then at the sidewalk again.

The bell rang and Caroline straightened her jacket. "See you," she smiled.

Joseph looked up at Caroline—or at least in her general direction—and muttered, "Okay."

Then Caroline turned to walk into school with Alma, who just stared in utter confusion.

✕

It wasn't something Caroline had given much thought to—the way black people went about their lives. They were always separate, and, considering what Joseph said to her, Caroline figured that they probably wanted it that way. The races didn't mix, she knew, but she never really knew why, or even spent much time wondering.

"You ever think about why whites and Negroes don't spend time together?" Caroline asked Alma after school. The two of them were walking to Alma's house, where Caroline was going to spend the rest of the afternoon.

"Not really, but Lewis sure does. Drives my parents mad."

Lewis. Alma's older brother. He was almost ten years older than Alma and had always been an object of fascination for Caroline. All the other older boys wore blazers and thin ties and they all had their hair swooped over with Brylcreem pomade. But not Lewis. He favored bulky wool sweaters and he had facial hair (sometimes just a mustache, sometimes a thin beard, sometimes a strange combination that covered his chin but not his jawline) and the hair on his head was shaggy and sometimes covered his ears. He was weird—all of Alma's friends knew that—but Caroline thought he was super nice.

When they got to Alma's house, Caroline was happy to see him. When she needed to use the bathroom, she passed Lewis's room and stopped, transfixed by the music from the record player and the posters of black musicians on his wall. This was not something you saw anywhere—you just didn't. Caroline imagined that the only other place you would see such things would be in the bedrooms of Negro kids across town, on their side of the city.

"That's Billie Holiday," Lewis said when he noticed Caroline standing there looking at one particular poster. The woman's eyes were closed and her mouth was wide open. She was singing into a microphone and her hair was tied back with a silk flower decorating the crown of her head. She wore a long elegant dress. Somehow, even in the midst of singing, even with her eyes closed, there was a sadness on her face, something weary and hard.

"Isn't that a woman?" Caroline asked.

Lewis laughed. "Of course it is."

"Billy's a boy's name."

Lewis's smile radiated sweetness. He put down his book. "Billie wasn't her real name. She was born Eleanora Fagan."

"Why'd she change it to a boy's name?"

"You know—I don't know why. But I do know that her voice is something sublime."

"Sublime? What's that?"

"Just listen." Lewis went to his record player. He picked up and then dropped the needle on the spinning disc. A few crackles and pops preceded a simple piano line and then a voice filled the air. It was odd, haunting; it never seemed to go up or down much. It just sort of skipped a bit above or below the music as she sang: "Southern trees bear a strange fruit

/ Blood on the leaves and blood at the root / Black bodies swinging in the southern breeze / Strange fruit hanging from the poplar trees."

Caroline stood there listening. And then came the end, just a few brief minutes later: "Here is fruit for the crows to pluck / For the rain to gather, for the wind to suck / For the sun to rot, for the trees to drop /Here is a strange and bitter crop."

While it played, Lewis sat very still, his eyes closed. Caroline watched him, the way he seemed transformed into somebody else. No longer the sweet guy who always said hello when she came over or the guy who kissed his sister on the head and said, "What's the story, Miss Glory?" when she walked through the door. Now, listening to the soulful woman with the man's name and the strange but haunting voice, he was a different person, withdrawn, moving into his own world. When it ended, he plucked the needle off the record and sat down.

"It sounds sad," Caroline said.

"It's about Negroes getting lynched."

Caroline had heard the word before but she didn't know what it meant.

"That's when white people hang a Negro by his neck from a tree until he's dead."

The tone in Lewis's voice was low but clearly angry, as if the words were squeezed out between clenched teeth.

Caroline frowned. "Why would anyone want to do that?"

"There are a lot of answers to that question, and none of them are good."

"I don't understand."

"I'm afraid I don't either."

It was getting confusing, and Caroline was feeling uncomfortable. She also remembered she needed to use the bathroom. But Lewis had been happy and smiling when she first walked by, and now he seemed upset. She couldn't help but feel that it was her fault somehow.

"There's a new Negro boy at school," she said, thinking, hoping, that perhaps this would make Lewis feel better.

It worked. He smiled. "Well, that is good. Integration is important. That's the only way. That's why I go to the Royal and the clubs down on Pennsylvania Avenue. It's important. At the clubs, people are decades ahead of the courts and the politicians."

Pennsylvania Avenue. Caroline had some idea that that was where the black businesses were. It was all the way across town, so far it might as well have been Pluto. But apparently Alma's brother went there. To Negro music clubs.

Caroline could hear Alma calling her, asking what she was doing, but she heard this only out of the corner of her consciousness for Lewis was still telling her about the clubs, throwing at her a whole list of names she'd never heard before. She kept nodding as he talked, as if she knew who these people were, and that if she didn't then at least she shouldn't admit it, not after seeing how excited he was about it, like maybe no one else he talked to cared one way or another.

"Ike Dixon and his house band, the Jazz Demons, the guys Duke Ellington called the city's best," Lewis was saying. "There's the Royal and the Sphinx and the Comedy Club. The guys who used to play there: Louis Armstrong, Charlie Parker. He's my favorite." Lewis pointed to the far wall, to a poster of a huge guy in a baggy suit blowing into a saxophone. "Fats Waller, Count Basie, Louis Jordan, Duke Ellington, Eubie Blake, Chick Webb, Cab Calloway."

Alma suddenly appeared behind Caroline. "What are you doing? I've been waiting."

"Hey Miss Glory," Lewis said to his sister.

Caroline knew Alma adored Lewis, but she also knew Alma thought he was weird. Alma looked in at the room, at the pictures on the walls, at the stray shirts and pants on his floor, at his record player, and made a face. "Come on," she said, tugging Caroline's arm.

"See you later," Lewis said. Then, moments later, the strange sounds of a high-pitched horn came floating out of his room.

9

WHEN CAROLINE WALKED into her house, her mother wasn't there to greet her at the door, so she made her way to the kitchen where the radio was going. It was loud, much louder than usual, and it seemed to boom off the walls.

"You are listening to the Mutual Broadcasting System's news report of the war in Korea. In a moment, we will hear the commentary of military analyst Major George Fielding Eliot, but first here is Supreme Commander of U.N. forces Gen. Matthew Ridgeway as he addresses a joint session of Congress."

Caroline stopped short when she saw her mother standing in the kitchen. Just standing, staring into space, a dish towel clutched in her hand and held near her face. She clearly hadn't noticed that Caroline had come in. She stood transfixed, listening to the broadcaster say, "sustained two of the severest attacks of the entire Korean campaign. Twice isolated far in advance of the general battle line, twice completely surrounded, in near zero weather—"

"Mama?"

Mrs. Panski jumped and dropped the towel. "Don't do that," she screeched. "You scared me half to death."

Caroline fetched the towel from the floor. "I'm sorry. I didn't mean to." She handed the towel to her mother. "That about Daddy?"

Mrs. Panski fairly lunged at the radio, snapping it off in one quick motion. "No, no. Of course not. Let's start your homework, okay?"

"OK."

"You want a glass of milk?"

"Sure."

Mrs. Panski rinsed a mug and filled it from the glass container in the icebox. Caroline noticed that her hand shook, just slightly. She got this way sometimes when she heard about Korea on the radio. Caroline was sure it was the reason why her mother was always turning the radio off, though she imagined that her mother listened during the day, when she was home alone. Caroline wanted to ask, but the topic was forbidden.

There were other ways to try and satisfy her curiosity about Korea. She discovered once when she was at the library that the *Baltimore Sun* ran stories about the war. She realized this quite by accident when she had to complete a current events assignment for Miss Bloom.

She picked up a copy of the paper and there, on the second page, was a photograph, taken in Korea, of two smiling soldiers, grimy with dirt, cigarettes hanging from their mouths. But smiling. Looking happy enough. She studied the picture for what felt like hours, days even, trying to imagine her father there, the two men standing along a ridge in front of a foxhole, just a hole in the ground, with sandbags all

around the opening. She read the photograph's caption, which explained that the men
were carrying a machine gun and a "3.5 rocket
launcher bazooka." Because the bazooka was
so big and so ugly, Caroline decided that her
dad, in his foxhole in Korea, had the machine
gun. And she imagined him looking much like
the guy in the photograph, with, as the caption
put it, "coils of ammo" wrapped in an X across
his shoulders.

She read the accompanying paragraph, explaining more about the weapons and how the
soldiers had to be especially vigilant because
in severe cold there was always the danger of a
jam, when the "lubrication in the guns gelled,"
and how the "springs on the firing pins" could
freeze up. Behind the foxhole, on the ridge of
the hill, the newspaper explained, were the
cylinders of "M-20 recoilless rifles."

But there was little else in the article, little
about the day-to-day lives of the soldiers.
And after a couple of weeks, Caroline no
longer bothered searching out newspapers.

The articles only offered more frustrations, and frustrations seemed to have the run of her days. She'd had enough of them. And she knew that asking her mother more questions would upset her and lead to, yes, more frustrations, on both their parts.

So, as her mother got her the promised glass of milk, Caroline changed subjects.

"Mama?"

"Yes?"

"Is it true that sometimes Negroes get hanged from trees?"

"Who on earth told you that?'

"Alma's brother."

"He the strange one?"

"He's nice."

"You're right. He is nice. But he is a little strange, too."

"Is what he said true?"

"Well, I suppose it is. Places south. Alabama. Mississippi."

"Not Maryland?"

"I should hope not."

"I told you there's a Negro boy in my class at school …"

"You did tell me that. Are you worried someone would do that to him?"

Caroline thought a moment. "Not really. But I wonder if maybe he worries about that. People aren't very friendly to him at school."

"Are you friendly to him?"

"I try to be. But he doesn't seem to like people talking to him. And he told me he hates it here, that if he had a choice he'd just stay in his neighborhood."

"I imagine it's difficult for him. Being the only Negro. He doesn't have the same kinds of freedoms you have."

Caroline knew better than to ask, but she couldn't help herself. "Is that what Daddy is doing in Korea?"

Mrs. Panski stiffened, the way she always did when Caroline asked questions about her father.

Caroline kept going. "Fighting for Negroes to have freedoms? Or Koreans, I mean. Before he left, he told me that sometimes part of being an American and having freedom is being called on to fight for others who aren't free."

Mrs. Panski's eyes watered. "He's right. Your father is right about that."

"Does Daddy fight with Negroes? I mean, other American soldiers who are Negro?"

"I don't know about that, Caroline. I really don't." Mrs. Panski unpacked Caroline's satchel. "We need to get to this homework, don't we?"

"Maybe I'll try to be Joseph's friend."

"Who's Joseph?"

"The Negro boy at school."

Mrs. Panski looked long and hard at her daughter.

"What?" Caroline asked. "Joseph seems like a nice boy. Besides, if Daddy can fight for freedom in Korea, I can fight for Joseph's freedom to make friends here at school."

"Just be careful, Caroline."

"What do you mean?"

Mrs. Panski looked off into space again, something she had been doing more and more of lately. "I don't know what I mean, sweetheart," she finally muttered. "I really don't."

Caroline tried to catch Joseph the next day before school. Once again, she left her house early, telling her friends the day before not to wait for her, but not telling them why. Images from Lewis's bedroom had been swimming in her head all night, as did the sounds of that big guy with the saxophone, and she figured this would be something she could talk to Joseph about. But then she realized that she couldn't even remember what Lewis had said the saxophone player's name was.

In any case, she stood alone on the steps for a half hour before groups of kids started showing up including, eventually, her friends. Caroline saw them coming and didn't want to have to answer their questions, so she stepped inside just at the moment she spotted Joseph walking alone along the sidewalk in the distance. She wanted desperately to wait for him, but she knew she couldn't without it looking strange. No one would understand.

During Geography she remembered. Billy Holiday. That was his name. She couldn't wait to talk to Joseph about him.

During lunch, she sat at her usual table with her friends. But when she noticed Joseph carrying his tray to his spot at his table, she headed over to him.

"Where are you going?" Beatrice asked after her.

Caroline didn't answer.

"Hey," she said when she got to Joseph.

He looked around before answering. "Hi."

"So, you know Billy Holiday?"

"Who?"

"Billy Holiday."

"That the blond kid in our class?"

"No, that's Billy Trethaway. Billy Holiday's a musician, plays saxophone. Sometimes I go

125

down to the clubs on Pennsylvania Avenue to see him play."

"Don't know him. But my uncle plays saxophone. Can play the cornet, too."

"Really? That's interesting. Can I sit?"

"Uh ..."

"Hey!" Caroline and Joseph turned. There stood Alan and two of his buddies.

"Don't answer them," Caroline instructed, though it appeared that Joseph had no intention of doing so anyhow.

"Don't you know that you're supposed to answer when someone talks to you?" one of the boys asked Joseph.

"Why don't you leave us alone?" Caroline said.

"Aw, isn't that sweet?" The boy turned to Joseph. "You get your girlfriend to fight your battles for you?"

Caroline turned red, partly from anger, partly from embarrassment. "I'm not his girlfriend," she spat at the same moment Joseph whispered, "She's not my girlfriend." His eyes looked wide and big and he suddenly appeared to Caroline a lot younger than she knew him to be.

Alan stepped closer, close enough to brush Caroline as he passed, and then stood hovering over Joseph. Alan paused, seemingly contemplating his next move, before sweeping Joseph's tray to the floor, spilling his food all over the place. A nasty looking stew, with chocolate milk spilling from its container and inundating Joseph's sandwich and French fries.

"Whoops," Alan said, a big dopey smile across his face. The other boys snickered.

Caroline wanted to punch them in the face. She could feel the heat crawling up her neck and spilling out over her collar. She wanted to kill them.

But Joseph remained calm. He didn't bother to pick up the food. But he didn't say a word to his tormentors, either. He simply stood and grabbed his books. But as he started to walk away, one of the other creeps poked the books from behind, causing them to spill out all over the floor. "Whoops again," he said.

Why isn't Joseph doing anything about it? Caroline thought. Why is he just taking it?

Whatever the reason, she wasn't going to take it. She wasn't going to just stand there. By this point, half the lunchroom had turned to watch. Something had to be done, and no one—not even the teachers—was doing anything about it. So, without thinking about what she was doing, Caroline turned to the jerk who had poked Joseph's books and slapped him in the face—hard. Instantly, a deep red imprint of Caroline's hand swelled up on the kid's face.

Stunned, the boy's jaw slacked and his eyes grew wide. He unconsciously placed his own hand where Caroline's had hit him. Then, as if finally realizing what had happened to him, his eyebrows creased into a sharp V and he pushed Caroline, sending her crashing against the table behind her. Two teachers came running over. The rest of the kids in the lunchroom rose from their seats, angling for a better look at the commotion, heading over to get nearer, ignoring the teachers yelling at them to sit down. The excitement was a tangible thing, zapping the entire room, at once filling the kids and emanating from them, each of them lucky enough to be witnessing this, to be able to have this exciting story to tell to friends later who hadn't seen it, or at home over supper to siblings and parents.

And then it got even better.

Caroline grabbed a milk carton from a girl sitting at the table where she'd just been pushed and, ignoring the girl's *Hey!*, threw it at the boy who pushed her, covering his entire face and most of his hair with milk. By the time the kid brushed it from his eyes, the teachers had grabbed both him and Caroline and had started escorting them out of the lunchroom and toward the principal's office.

Caroline's eyes and face burned at this public and embarrassing display. But the worst part was that when she looked back, she realized that Joseph had just stood there the whole time. He hadn't even bothered to come to her defense. He hadn't done anything.

What she did, she did for him, and now she was going to get in trouble.

When it was her turn with Principal Podolski, Caroline sat in the chair in front of his desk with her arms crossed over her chest, still fuming about what had taken place.

"I just don't understand it, Miss Panski. You are probably the last one at this school I would expect this behavior from."

Caroline didn't say a word.

"Now, I am going to let you off with a warning. I know the circumstances with your father and—"

Caroline felt a burn behind her eyes, the tears that threatened to spill. But she blinked and swallowed it back. She would not cry. "It's not that," she choked out.

"What then?"

"What about those boys? Shouldn't they be in trouble? What they did to Joseph?"

"Caroline—" Principal Podolski folded his hands on his desk, wrapping his fingers around one another into a tight ball. "I'm not certain I understand why you are concerning yourself so much with Joseph."

"Why shouldn't I? No one else cares."

"I'm not necessarily saying you shouldn't care. But it is not accurate to say that no one else does. He is here under special circumstances. His father died in South Carolina and he has moved to Baltimore and we are experimenting with integration in some small cases."

"I saw some Negroes at the high school."

"Yes. A-listers. What I'm telling you is that perhaps you're taking on more than you might wish to chew."

"What I know is that my Daddy is fighting in Korea so that other people can have freedom. And it only seems right that people here should have freedom, too. Like the freedom to not be bullied. To be able to sit wherever they like in the lunchroom. To have whatever friends they want to."

Principal Podolski sat back in his chair, leaning so far it looked like he might topple over. "I'm not certain I see an apt comparison there. But I respect what you're saying. And I certainly respect what your father is doing. I fought in World War II myself." He paused and let out a long sigh. "You are free to go."

Caroline rose from her chair and gathered her satchel. "Am I in trouble?"

"No. But Miss Panski?"

"Yes?"

"I want to be clear that there will be no more milk throwing in my lunchroom. Is that understood?"

"Yes, sir."

"Wait until it becomes an Olympic sport, and then you can throw all the milk you want."

Caroline smiled. "Yes, sir."

She made her way back to the lunchroom and when she arrived, just a few minutes before dismissal, the place went dead quiet, everyone staring in her direction like she was some new creature no one knew, or cared to know. Even Alma, Beatrice, and Genevieve stared.

Caroline tried her best to ignore everyone. But when she saw Joseph looking at her, too, she felt angry again. She marched up to him. "What is wrong with you?" she asked.

"What do you mean? What are you angry with me for?"

"You just sat there while I got in trouble."

"I never asked you to come to my rescue."

"But no one else was."

Joseph grabbed his books and got up. "I don't need you to fight my battles for me."

"But you were just sitting there."

"You don't understand. People like me? We don't get to hit back. Hit back, we get killed."

"You don't know what I understand and what I don't."

"Believe me, you don't understand," Joseph said and collected his books before adding, "And you never will."

Then he left Caroline standing there, alone, in the middle of the room, with everyone else staring in open-mouthed silence. She wanted to scream, throw more milk, throw whatever. She hated them, hated them all. Hated everything.

But very quickly, and very much against her will, the anger turned to something else and before she could even realize it, tears were flowing down her cheeks, like someone had turned on a spigot with no turn-off valve. She ran from the room, out into the hallway, and then right out of the school.

10

CAROLINE TRIED HER BEST the next day to act as if everything was still normal, as if she hadn't made a spectacle of herself in front of everyone the day before. She left for school early to avoid her friends since she just couldn't bear to see them, or anyone, really. In her classroom, her level of concentration was intense. She made her best effort not to look anywhere but to the front of the class. It made no difference that Joseph continually looked her way—something Beatrice eventually took notice of. To no avail. She was not looking back at him. She was not looking at anyone.

She remained quiet during lunch, too, only muttering "Nothing" when the other girls asked her what was going on. Eventually, they tired of asking and just ignored her, something she was grateful for.

Even on the walk home she remained silent, lost in a reverie, the sounds of her friends chattering away merely a wash of noise.

Until she heard Beatrice's voice, clear and loud, above all the others: "How long, Miss Caroline, before you start speaking to us again?"

She didn't mean to inflame Beatrice, but when Caroline shrugged in response, Beatrice obviously took it as an intentional dig, a suggestion that Caroline might never speak to any of them again.

"Well, it sure is rude. And annoying."

"Lay off," Genevieve said.

"I'm not certain how long we have to take her acting this way. I'm sorry, Caroline," Beatrice said. "It just seems you have more of an interest in talking to the new nigger boy than to us. That hurts, Caroline. How are we to feel if you act like you hate us?"

Caroline couldn't respond. She had no obligation to anyone and anyway, this was the way

Beatrice had acted for years—involving herself in something inexcusable and then twisting it in such a way that it seemed like it was your fault. Besides, Beatrice was right. Caroline did have more of an interest in Joseph than she did in her own friends, even if she would never put it as meanly as Beatrice had.

But she couldn't say this to Beatrice, or to anyone. She didn't have the words for these sentiments because she didn't understand them. At least she couldn't understand them except as fuzzy feelings bubbling to the surface at arbitrary times and filling her with a mixture of anger and sadness and hurt.

At their separation point, she bid her friends goodbye—her only words to them—and didn't even register Beatrice's face turning red, the anger leaking out of her so much she was rendered speechless. Alma walked home beside her in silence.

Caroline repeated her avoidance tactic the next morning, leaving before her friends could join her. In school, the other students still cast wary looks her way. But by lunchtime this had stopped, replaced by something far more meaningful. A sense of deep expectation pervaded the classroom. Miss Bloom looked at the clock. The students stared, wide-eyed, expectant, big smiles plastered on their faces. The clock ticked its way toward 3:00 p.m.

"Have a Merry Christmas and Happy New Year," Miss Bloom said. "And please don't forget to keep the less fortunate in your prayers."

The bell rang and the students ran out of the classroom. Caroline was far more composed. Amidst the chaos of fleeing students, Joseph caught her eye and smiled. Caroline couldn't help herself. She smiled back. It felt good. It seemed like ages since she'd smiled.

The students burst out of the school, screaming and running. At the back of the procession came Caroline and Joseph, preceded by Beatrice, Alma, and Genevieve.

Caroline turned to Joseph: "Have a nice break," she said.

"You do the same."

The two of them lingered—a bit too long.

Alma, Beatrice, and Genevieve waited. While Alma and Genevieve talked, Beatrice looked up at the top of the stairs. "Caroline!" she yelled with obvious impatience.

"Gotta go," Caroline said.

"Bye." Joseph started down the sidewalk.

Caroline called after him, "See you next year."

Joseph smiled.

Beatrice glared, and this time Caroline took real notice. Joseph, she decided, was worth a lot of things. But worth losing her best friends? That was a tough one.

11

A SMALL DUSTING of snow softened the building's hard brick edges. Just a few blocks and a whole world away, the boys played hockey, their shouts ricocheting off the nearby buildings. In her room, Caroline lay on her bed reading a book while downstairs Mrs. Panski made pancake batter and scrambled eggs. A teapot whistled on the stove.

Though school had stopped for winter break, the rest of the world went on. After breakfast, Caroline walked along the sidewalk, passing the two men on their stoops. They waved and she returned an unenthusiastic wave. She came to the alley that led to the frozen pond, hesitated, and then turned back around, back toward home. She didn't much feel like hockey. Whereas once it had been her outlet, her joy, her everything, now she couldn't really muster the energy to do much of anything. The excitement she usually had when she thought about playing hockey just wasn't there. She spent the rest of her day mostly in her room, silent, brooding. No one in the house spoke much, each settling into his or her own private world. Despite the closeness of the quarters, Caroline, Sam, and Mrs. Panski managed to keep entirely clear of one another.

Beautiful spent much of the morning in a prolonged fight with her coughs and dry heaves. The Panskis had seen this before and they no longer thrust their fingers in her mouth to extract whatever it was they believed must have been stuck up there. When he was younger, Sam used to give the dog spoonfuls of peanut butter and then watched with glee as Beautiful spent the next twenty minutes licking furiously at the top of her mouth—head tilted, tongue spinning like a top, her little beard soaked and dripping. Sam called it "yakking" and he couldn't get enough of this entertainment until Mrs. Panski forbade it and told him that what he was doing amounted to torturing the poor animal. At that Sam wept and held onto Beautiful, apologizing over and over again until Mrs. Panski told him that it wasn't really torture, that it was just something she said to get him to stop, and that in fact the dog loved peanut butter. But to stop doing it nonetheless.

But now Beautiful was yakking again, her head tilted in that little dance. But this time it wasn't food that brought it on. In fact, it seemed to come out of nowhere, the coughs and yaks, before subsiding on their own. Then she would she lay peacefully on the floor next to one of the family.

After supper, Mrs. Panski sat in her chair in the front room, flipping through a magazine. It was well past the kids' bedtimes, but she said nothing, and neither of the children questioned it. Sam sat on the carpet working in a coloring book and trying to ignore Beautiful pawing at him. Finally he looked up and Beautiful flopped on her back for a belly rub. The radio played in the background.

"And so we bid goodbye to 1952 and welcome a new year. President Truman will celebrate in Washington, D.C. with a small ceremony at the White House before heading to Missouri for a presidential vacation. Due to the estrangement between President Truman and the man who will succeed him in the presidency in twenty days, General Dwight David Eisenhower, the two have spoken little about transitional matters. Perhaps in the new year."

Downtown, the department stores tried to outdo one another. They decked their street windows with elaborate Christmas displays designed to draw customers inside. And there were plenty of customers. Caroline's dad had explained to her about the post-World War II economic boom and when she, Sam, and her mother walked amidst the throngs on Charles and St. Paul, Howard and North streets, it appeared everything was still booming. War, it seemed, could mean jobs and a humming economy. Her dad had even said that job security was one of the reasons he joined the army. But if she had a vote, Caroline would choose tough times and no war. She'd choose to have her dad back.

Neighborhood churches also did a brisk business. Packed to the gills with congregants, some of the old-timers and more fervent among them sniffed with indignation at the sudden appearance of those who only showed up at Christmas and Easter.

In the Panskis' neighborhood, rowhomes were festooned with festive lights, and pass-ersby could see tall, gaily decorated trees through the front bow windows of most of the houses. And from the outside, Caroline's house looked no different from any of the others on the street. They had strung no lights, that was true (that had always been Mr. Panski's job), but they had a tree and, though without much chatter and with suppressed enthusiasm, had decorated it with ornaments and tinsel.

On Christmas morning, the Panskis made a courageous show of it, but it was a decidedly uncheerful Christmas. There was no way around it. From the mantel, a framed picture of David Panski looked down upon them. They exchanged modest gifts and smiled when they opened them, but a palpable sadness pervaded everything. Several times Mrs. Panski wiped her eyes with a tissue and then smiled bravely for the benefit of the kids. But they weren't fooled.

After they'd exchanged presents, Caroline went outside. She walked down the sidewalk, her skates over her shoulder. She'd try it. Skate a bit. Maybe that would make her feel better. There was no one else outside. It seemed the entire population of the city was cloistered inside their homes.

There was something pleasing about the solitude. Caroline walked briskly, managing to feel a little less glum with every step. As she passed a narrow break between rows of homes, an odd hissing sound startled her:

"Pssst."

Caroline yelped, jumped, and turned toward the sound, all at once. There was Joseph, emerging from the shadows.

"What on earth are you doing here?" Caroline asked, her heart pounding in her chest. "You scared me half to death."

"Figured you weren't scared of anything."

"What would make you say that?"

"The way you stood up to those boys."

Caroline smiled in spite of herself. "They deserved it."

"I don't disagree with that. Look, I'm sorry. I should have helped you."

"It's okay. But, why didn't you help?"

"I told you. I can't. I just have to take it."

"And do nothing?"

Joseph nodded.

"You ever think of quitting?"

"I can't do that either."

"Why not?"

"Because my Granny would kill me for one thing."

Caroline smiled. "So, what are you doing here anyway? I thought you told me you live up Preston way."

"I do."

"Say, you here looking for me?"

Joseph didn't say anything. He looked away. But before he did, Caroline could clearly see the blood rising in his cheeks. Despite the cold, he looked, suddenly, rather overheated.

"Sorry," she mumbled. There followed a long awkward silence. "Shouldn't you be at home? It's Christmas," she added, trying to change the subject to spare him any more embarrassment.

"My Granny is a Jehovah's witness," he said.

"What's that?"

"I'm not even sure I can explain it right. But I do know that we don't celebrate Christmas on account of it."

"You're not Christian?"

"We are. Jehovah's witnesses are Christians. They just don't celebrate Christmas is all. And in my house, what Granny says goes."

Caroline looked up and down the streets. "You sure you should be here?"

"I'm not scared. I got you to protect me."

Caroline smiled again. So did Joseph. "So you're not still mad at me?"

Joseph shook his head. "Never said I was mad. Are you mad at me?"

"Nope."

For a fleeting moment, their eyes locked before they both quickly looked away.

When Caroline looked back up, she saw that Joseph was freezing, his arms wrapped around his chest. He blew into his bare hands.

"Where's your jacket?"

Joseph plucked the sides of his thin cover.

"That's no winter jacket."

"It's what I have."

"You must be freezing."

Joseph shrugged. "I'm all right."

"You wanna see the rink?" Caroline asked.

"What's that?"

"Where you play hockey, silly. Course, it's not a real rink. Just a froze-over pond down the way."

"I've never seen hockey. Never heard of it until you told me."

Caroline shook her head, mystified.

"I like football."

"Football's okay. But hockey is even better. Fastest thing on skates. My mom used to play."

"Your mother?"

Caroline nodded, smiled, and grabbed Joseph by the hand—mitten on skin—and dragged him down the street.

When Caroline and Joseph arrived at the edge of the pond, Joseph just stood there and gawked, as if it was the first time he'd ever laid eyes on something so amazing, like the pond was the ocean or the Grand Canyon or something equally immense and impressive.

Caroline studied him. "You've never seen ice before?"

"Not this big."

"There's no ice in South Carolina?"

"Unh-uh. Not like this."

Caroline gently pushed Joseph out onto the slick surface. But even a gentle push proved too much. He slid and slipped and then fell flat.

Caroline laughed through her mittens. "You okay?"

"I'm okay."

Caroline offered her hand. Joseph took it and she helped him up. Except that he kept slipping and eventually pulled her to the ice next to him. They both laughed.

She saw that his teeth were chattering. "Here," she said. "Take this." She handed him her scarf.

"I don't need it."

She wrapped it around his neck anyway.

"Thanks."

"Now watch how it's done. It's easy."

Caroline laced up her skates and took off for the far edge of the pond. For once, she forgot about hockey. This was figure skating—good figure skating. Caroline skated in tight circles, lifted a leg, outstretched her arms, across the ice and back again—putting on quite a graceful show.

Joseph watched her as she made her way across the ice, a big, wide smile plastered across his face.

It was late afternoon and there was still light in the sky as Joseph and Caroline walked toward her house. Every now and again, she looked up and around, both ways down the street as if something discomfited her.

"You all right?" he asked.

"Yeah, I'm all right."

"It's on account of me being colored."

"No—"

"If my Granny knew I was here, she'd take a switch to my hide."

"Sounds like she's real protective of you. I guess that means she loves you a lot."

"She's just mean is all." Caroline laughed, and Joseph did, too. "I guess it means she loves me, too. But she can be mean."

"I used to think that about my mama, but really she's nice. Just doing her job, I guess."

"That's what mamas are born to do. You going to be one someday?"

Caroline shrugged.

"I bet you'd be a good one."

She blushed, looking away up the street again, and saw a man staggering toward them. He was dressed atrociously with his hat askew and threatening to slip from his head, his coat a mess of rips and tears, his pants shredded at the bottom so much that they looked tasseled. He tottered too close to Joseph and Caroline, swaying just near them. The two kids stepped back, stunned, unable to run, or unsure what they should do.

The man smiled, a grin at first beatific but suddenly cold, cruel, and mocking.

"Little lady," he said, his breath ripe with the smell of some very strong liquor, "Whatcha doin' with this here nigger?" The man turned an accusing finger toward Joseph. "Nigger boy, whatcha doin' with this here white girl? Your kind been lynched for such offenses."

The man produced a bottle wrapped in newspaper from the pocket of his filthy coat, took a deep swig, and turned to Caroline. He grabbed her elbow. "Come on, missy. I'll take you home. Nigger boy, you best go on back where's you came from unless you want to invite a lynching."

Caroline twisted her arm away from the man, but his grip tightened.

"Mister, you best let go a her."

"Or else what, boy?"

Joseph kicked the man in his shin, hard, grabbed Caroline's hand, and the two of them took off down the street.

"Here, this way," Caroline said, steering Joseph toward an alley that she knew was a short cut.

Just before they entered the alley, she looked back to see the man sitting in a filthy puddle in the street, kneading his shin and shouting curses.

When they emerged on the other side of the alley, they stopped, taking in deep gulps of air, their fears turning into nervous titters as they collected themselves.

"Thank you," Caroline said.

"He had a hold of you. I couldn't just stand there. You would have done the same for me."

Caroline nodded. After another moment, they continued on, in silence.

A stew churned inside Caroline, as if the world was moving too quickly for her, each moment presenting one more thing she couldn't hope to understand. Everything suddenly looked unfamiliar. It was the same old sky, same old street, same old stoop, except it all looked different, as if some giant hand had come along and smudged the edges of everything.

When Caroline and Joseph approached the Panski house, they stopped short of the front steps.

"This is me here," Caroline said.

Joseph appraised the house. "It's nice."

Caroline shrugged. "You sure you're going to be okay heading home?"

"I know the safe routes now. Besides, you and me are the only ones out except that old crazy man."

"Please be careful."

"If he came round again, I'd kick him in his other shin."

Caroline didn't laugh. "I'm serious."

"I'd run. He'd never catch me. Not with all that liquor sloshing round his gut."

"That's a way better plan." Caroline looked to her house, back to Joseph, and to the house again. "Well, Merry Christmas," she said.

"Merry Christmas to you, too."

"I guess I'll see you in school."

"Yeah. See you next year."

Caroline started up the steps, then hesitated, turned, ran back down, planted a kiss on Joseph's cheek, and then sprinted back up, leaving Joseph glowing on the sidewalk, his fingers touching the spot where Caroline kissed him.

Before Caroline could get to the door, though, it flew open. Joseph took off down the street, Caroline's scarf still wrapped around his neck.

"Get in here!" Mrs. Panski growled.

Caroline's stomach did somersaults as she stepped inside. She knew she'd done wrong and her will to fight, for the moment, left her completely.

"Sit!" her mother commanded.

Caroline sat. She felt small and vulnerable, huddled in a chair as Mrs. Panski paced before her. Beautiful, curled on the rug nearby, raised her head to watch.

"Where do you know that boy from?" Mrs. Panski demanded.

"That's Joseph, from school. I told you, we're friends."

"I saw what you did. Do you not think I didn't see you? Do you not think that the whole street couldn't see you?"

"There was nobody out on the street. And besides, I'm allowed to give my friend a goodbye kiss on the cheek."

"You are? Says who?"

Beautiful, suddenly spooked by the loud voices and tension, ran into another room.

"It doesn't mean anything."

"Caroline, do you hear yourself? You were kissing a Negro boy in the middle of the street, in the wide open, and you're telling me it doesn't mean anything? Just where do you think you live? Who do you think you are?"

Caroline fought back tears. "I don't care if he's a Negro—"

"It's not natural," Mrs. Panski interrupted. Then she softened her tone, searching for the right way to explain. "People should stick with their own kind. You understand that, don't you?"

"No, I don't understand that at all." She stood up and wiped her nose on her sleeve. "He's a sweet boy. I like him, and I want him to be my friend."

"Oh, Caroline. What am I to do with you?" Mrs. Panksi watched as her daughter ran up the stairs, bolting past Sam who'd been listening from the landing the whole time.

The sound of a slamming door followed.

"She's sure in trouble, isn't she, Mama?" Sam asked, smiling at the prospect.

"Hush your mouth, Samuel Panski."

12

WHY DID THE WORLD have to be this way? Why couldn't she just be friends with who she wanted to be friends with? Unfortunately for Caroline, whenever she got into these states before bed, it was almost inevitable that her dreams that evening would follow a predictable pattern. It would only be a matter of time before images of her father would overcome all her defenses and dominate her dreamscape.

So, as she had before on many occasions, she battled against sleep, knowing her brain was overloaded with everything she knew of her dad and Korea, from the newsreels and the radio broadcasts, and from the letters he wrote.

She couldn't help herself. When she thought of him, despite what cheery things he wrote in his letters to her, she couldn't help but picture the worst—the strange, bleak landscape, the cold, the loneliness. She knew he had the family photograph with him, the one with Caroline's mom in her summer dress, that beautiful smile of hers, and Sam and Caroline, his adoring children. She'd picture his grimy fingers holding it and imagined that he'd probably want to stare at it all day if he could. But she knew also that there were other soldiers around and they'd probably be constantly interrupting him. He'd written to her about his two best friends, Lundeberg and Wysocki, and how they loved hockey, too, just like she did.

"What do you think about that?" he wrote to her. "I told them my daughter could probably kill 'em out on the ice."

She wondered if he knew that her mom had told her that she used to play. She wondered also if he told Lundeberg and Wysocki that, too, or if maybe he'd be embarrassed by that, that they'd think she was some kind of monster or something. Of course, he'd only have to show them the picture and they'd see that wasn't true. Her mom was beautiful.

Her eyes closed against her will. She snapped her head up, trying to keep herself awake, but it wouldn't take. Eventually she'd have to fall asleep. The tide of it was coming on strong, and her lids were drooping until she couldn't fight it any longer.

Caroline had good reason to be wary for it was a terrible dream. Her dad was in that same place, with the mountains and the cold and the foxhole. In the far distance came the sound of explosions. Then loud booms echoed across the skies, louder and louder, coming closer and closer until *WHUMP!* A massive crater kicked up close to where her dad and the other men stood.

He had to get in his foxhole. He grabbed his gun, readied, and started firing. Even in the dream it was loud, so loud you couldn't think. The enemy came in great swarms. It looked like someone had stepped on an anthill and sent a million of them scurrying in every direction.

The coils of ammunition were wrapped across her father's shoulders and chest and they rapidly disappeared as the bullets fed into his machine gun. No matter how much he fired, there was a new wave of enemy soldiers bearing down on him. They just kept coming. And they had their guns and they were firing away, too. And all of that firing, with its whizzes and whistles and booms and cracks, created a smoke-filled sky, so thick no one could see a thing.

Caroline's father tried to fire more, but his gun jammed. Frantic, he tried to fix it, but he couldn't get it to work. He peered out of his hole. There, just off to his right, were six of his fellow soldiers, hugging the ridge line, firing away and fighting for their lives. One of them was crouched, holding his hands on the side of his head, fingers plugged into his ears. The smoke enveloped them, the guns' long spent cylinders stacked along the hillside.

And then Caroline's father stopped. Stopped firing, stopped yelling. Just stopped. He looked out over the far hills, where the smoke had miraculously cleared, and a feeling of peace came over the whole scene. It was beautiful, if you looked at it right. The trees had no leaves, not with winter and weapons stealing them. But they were left with long slender branches that shook and shuddered in the heat of war and, somehow, were beautiful.

The men nearby were screaming at him. One of the soldiers was just near him, crawling toward the hole and screaming, screaming, screaming. His eyes were wide and terror-filled. It was Tyler, the quiet kid from New Mexico. But now he was screaming, and he was tugging on Caroline's dad's uniform, pulling him, trying to get him out of the hole.

But he just stood there, paralyzed. That's when everything became completely quiet. The men were still firing; the bombs were still dropping; the screams were still piercing the air. But you couldn't hear anything. Like in some vacuum. And nothing changed in that stillness until Caroline's father looked down and there, on the muddy, bloody ground next to his boots, he saw it, the grenade that had come rolling into his hole.

But by the time he tried to climb out, it was too late.

BOOM!

CAROLINE GASPED AND sprung up in bed, her hair a sweaty mop plastered to her head, her pillow wet, too. She was crying, and didn't know why. She'd had a dream, yes, but she couldn't immediately recall what it had been about. She knew only that it had been terrible, that it would probably cling to her and gnaw at her and leave her with a deep, empty pit in her stomach.

Still in the grasp of sleepiness, she slowly realized that there was a strange noise, and it was in her room, right next to her, in fact. She finally realized it was Beautiful. The dog had been sleeping in her room, but was now yakking and yakking. It was a terrible sound, different this time from the others, edged with something malevolent. When Caroline collected herself, she realized that her mother was in the room, too.

"Where is she?" Mrs. Panski asked.

"Who?"

"Beautiful. Where is she?" Mrs. Panski repeated, flipping on the light, still in the fog of her own recent sleep. When the light came on, Caroline saw her mother's hair was in wild disarray, her gauzy robe half-on, her eyes puffy. Bewildered, Caroline sat on the edge of her bed, her eyes trying to open fully but blinking back the obtrusive light.

And then they spotted Beautiful hunched against the closet, her body prone but her neck high in the air. She looked up at them, but continued her horrible honking. She inhaled through her nose, sucking in gulps of air, but each gulp brought on a new coughing fit that quickly degenerated into wheezing and choking.

"Mama, something's wrong with her," Caroline said.

Mrs. Panski started toward Beautiful, but Caroline got there first. Caroline scooped the dog into her arms and peppered her face with kisses. She pulled back only when Beautiful responded with violent snuffles, blowing strands of moisture from her nose.

Caroline looked up at her mother. "What do we do?"

"I don't know."

Beautiful endured another round of violent, spasmodic coughing before dropping her head to the floor. She looked exhausted, ready to give up the big fight. It was a battle, Caroline could tell that now. Beautiful could no longer breathe properly. She inhaled violently, like slurping her life through a straw. After several more coughing fits, she was too tired to even lift her head. Caroline curled up beside her and kept her hands on the dog, petting and whispering and singing to her. There was nothing else she could do but just be there and love her.

Mrs. Panski knelt beside Caroline. There was little suspense. Beautiful could not keep it up for much longer. She slowly wound down, like turning off a series of switches. She took a few last shallow inhalations, and then she was gone. Caroline buried her face in Beautiful's fur and wept.

Beautiful had greeted Caroline with licks and tail wags when her parents first brought her home from the hospital. She'd been in the house Caroline's whole life, and now, just like that, she was gone. One more hurt in a universe full of them.

Dawn arrived. They'd spent the previous hours huddled in Caroline's room, alternately holding Beautiful, kissing her, crying. At certain moments, the crying became deep and intense and, while unacknowledged, it became clear that they were crying not only over this absence, this separation, but another, too. And while a dog's departure from this life could not compare to a father's and husband's absence,

Beautiful's death felt somehow unnaturally cruel and they mourned the harder for it.

Mrs. Panski retrieved an old bedsheet that she had previously cut to make rags, and they wrapped up Beautiful, swaddled like a newborn baby, immediately rendering their beloved pet into little more than a series of folds and creases that bore little resemblance to the animal inside. Once secured there, Beautiful took on a weight she simply didn't possess in life. When Sam stumbled into the room and saw her under the sheet, he knew immediately and started to cry.

The funeral was a simple affair, conducted in their postage stamp back yard. Surprising his sister and his mother, Sam took the lead. He acted as if he'd decided that Beautiful's death marked the moment he needed to step up and be the man of the house. He pulled on a patch of dead grass in the corner of the yard near a divot just under a collapsing portion of wooden fencing where Beautiful, in her more vigorous years, used to dig and claw at some unseen thing on the other side of the fence or buried deep in the ground. The permanent divot was a reminder of her, and the space felt like the obvious place in which to lay her.

After clearing the dormant grass, Sam employed his father's old shovel, making quick work of the soil, damp from an evening shower. Mrs. Panski watched her son, admiration on her face. She looked around at the yard, at the deplorable condition of it. They'd let the place go since David had gone off to war, and only the winter weather kept it from being an absolute riot of unchecked growth.

It had always been David's space to maintain, and he'd taken a certain pleasure in it that he masked with frustration and, sometimes, anger, returning from a Saturday afternoon session of beating back the vines and weeds with muttered curses. But he'd grab a glass of water and then get right back out there, pulling and tugging and clipping and edging with vigor. He'd then run the push mower over it all, hitting it so low and tight that for a few days after, one would be hard pressed to identify what was grass and what were weeds. One year, he even planted a small garden. But the bounty was three withered pea pods, a tomato that some nocturnal critters attacked and ate, and half a dozen malformed zucchini. And that was the end of the Panski garden.

Seeing Sam work so vigorously in the yard brought a bittersweet smile to Mrs. Panski's lips. It was a lovely sight, a preview, perhaps, of the man Sam would become.

He reached out for the bundle. Caroline held Beautiful to her chest for one last squeeze and handed it over. Sam gently placed the dog in the ground. He got up and all three stood in the cold silent morning for a few moments, not saying anything, staring at the hole, at the sheet, at the dog inside. And then Sam piled the dirt back on. He lovingly swept his hands over the fresh mound, patting it in place and leveling it. But he left the divot intact. A patch where the grass would not grow so well. A reminder.

14

THINGS HAD IMPROVED a bit at school, but now, after Beautiful's death, Caroline reverted to quiet Caroline, withdrawn Caroline, residing in a private space that most allowed her to inhabit. But during lunch, impatient Beatrice demanded to know what it was now that caused Caroline to shun her friends. "My dog died," she whispered, and her eyes grew heavy with moisture.

Alma and Genevieve sat quietly. Alma put her hand on Caroline's shoulder and gave it a rub. Even Beatrice softened a bit. Until just before the bell, that is, when she noticed Caroline once again looking toward Joseph, wrapping up his lunch alone at his table on the far end of the cafeteria. Caroline's eyes tracked Joseph all the way across the room as he got up and dumped the detritus of his lunch in the can. Anyone paying any attention could have seen. She was just so obvious about it. Beatrice stood suddenly. She didn't even say goodbye to any of her friends, just snatched up her marbled notebook from the table and left.

Caroline couldn't shake Beautiful from her thoughts. She heard Beautiful's peculiar noises in the squeaks of her classmates' chairs against the linoleum floors, in the din of their voices in the cafeteria, in the squeal of tires along the streets. And she saw the dog not only in her mind's eye, but as a corporeal creature, fully alive and darting here and there just beyond the periphery of her vision.

So it was not a terrible shock to Caroline when she actually did see Beautiful while walking home one day. The resemblance was remarkable. If she didn't know Beautiful had died, she would have sworn that was her dog huddled up just on the lip of an alley, shaking and chattering, its little haunches curled up underneath her.

Caroline walked toward the dog. "Hi, sweetie," she said, walking slowly, holding out her hand. The dog didn't react at first, but just watched, warily. Then she cocked her head before shuffling back a few inches.

Caroline continued toward her, hand open, voice soothing.

The dog raised its lip. It shook violently now, its little teeth bared, the ragged fur on its head quivering. And then it struck, uncoiling itself from its pathetic position and snapping down hard on Caroline's finger. The dog let out a shriek as it bit her, some hideous, unnatural sound that sprang from its mouth at the very moment it chomped down on Caroline's finger, muffling and amplifying the sound all at once.

Caroline yelped and pulled back. Her finger throbbed with pain and she held it upright as pearls of blood formed over the teeth marks. The dog, lost, scared, and confused, took off. Caroline watched as it tore away, bounding right into the street just as a huge tail-finned Ford turned the corner. Caroline saw the bushy tail, the spots of gray in the fur, the little, almost stunted legs. Of course it wasn't Beautiful, her precious dog, dead now and buried in the backyard. This was some lookalike masquerading as her beloved pet. And now Caroline had to watch this other poor creature breathe its last, just as she'd had to watch her own sweetie do the same.

The Ford rolled right over the dog. It didn't stop or even slow, the driver completely unaware of the creature below. Caroline cried out, and then her heart flipflopped as she watched the dog emerge, amazingly, on the other side of the car, fully intact, and still running, before disappearing through another alley on the far side of the road.

The pain in her finger doubled. She pressed it, hoping to stanch the flow of blood. But pressing it made it hurt more, so she walked with it stretched out in front of her, squeezing just below the knuckle, and watching as the finger turned from a scarlet red to a strange white and then a bluish color that made her hurry, just a bit more, toward home.

When she got home, she knocked and stood there, frozen. Mrs. Panski opened the door and saw Caroline holding her bloodied finger out in front of her.

"What happened?" Mrs. Panski asked, her voice edged with alarm.

"I saw a dog that looked just like Beautiful. I went to pet her—"

Caroline did an admirable job of holding back a crying jag. Mrs. Panski could see it in Caroline's face, the blood thrumming just below the surface, the tears just behind her glossy eyes. She held her daughter close and didn't ask for an explanation. She could figure it out. Anyone could. She held her tighter still and Caroline submitted. Allowed herself to be swallowed up by her mother. It didn't matter if they got blood on their clothes. At this moment, in this breathing-space of time, all either of them needed to know was that they were not alone. They had each other. And that could not and would not change.

After Mrs. Panski soothed her daughter, she poured antiseptic on the cut and then bandaged it up. They sat for some time, Caroline calming all the while.

"I was just about to go to the grocer's. Sam is at a friend's this afternoon. Why don't you come with me?"

Caroline nodded. She liked the idea of being with her mother today, felt they needed each other. She knew her mother was still upset about the situation with Joseph out on the street, but in the wake of Beautiful's death, the subject hadn't come up again and Caroline knew better than to do anything to remind her mother of it. She surely had enough to worry about. Beautiful's death had been a blow to everyone, but perhaps the most for Mrs. Panski.

Caroline knew her parents had gotten the puppy not long after they were married and had moved into their new home. And her absence now was a thing much heavier than her presence had been. She was a small dog and often quiet, content to lie curled up at someone's feet for hours at a time. But with her gone, it felt like a cavern had opened up in the house. The quiet dog's absence made this new quiet something much larger and profound. Caroline knew that for her mother, Beautiful was yet one more reminder of her husband.

Caroline watched her mother in the grocery. It seemed that walking the aisles allowed Mrs. Panski to enter into a kind of reverie of distraction. She took her time reading labels, comparing one product to another, even though, as far as Caroline knew, she hardly ever gave a thought to these things before.

Price had always been the primary concern. Now, ingredients, ounces, even the colors on the packages—all these, it seemed, consumed her, allowed her to linger and not return so soon to their empty-feeling home, a place without comforting noises. Caroline retreated into neighboring aisles, occasionally peeking over at her mother, watching her, sensing that she needed some space to be alone with her private thoughts.

Mrs. Panski had been staring at a can of Ajax cleanser, lost in the red and blue swoop on the can, when a man passed behind her. It seemed something told her to look up and when she did, she froze. She stared at the man. Caroline did, too, sensing something troubling about him. He didn't look dangerous, just an older man in a bowler hat and a blazer with a can of shaving cream in his hand.

The man looked over, perhaps sensing he was being watched. When he looked up, his face softened. He smiled and made his way over toward Caroline's mother.

"Eloise Weatherbee?" he said.

"Hello," Mrs. Panski replied.

"Well, I'll be. How on earth are you, Eloise?"

"It's actually Panski now."

"Sure, of course. No chance a woman like you could remain unmarried for long."

Caroline's mother blushed.

"Well, it sure is nice to see you, Eloise," he said, and he moved closer to her, his hand outstretched, as if he was about to touch her.

Caroline watched as her mother stepped backward and then dropped her can of Ajax on the floor, where the top opened and the white powder spilled and plumed all over, covering the man's shoes. She stuttered, "I'm so sorry. Excuse me," and then ran out of the store, abandoning all her groceries in the process.

"Mama?" Caroline squealed, and ran out after her.

She caught up to her mother on the sidewalk and placed her hand in hers. Mrs. Panski reacted by jerking her hand away and then, realizing it was Caroline, looked at her as if she had forgotten they were even together, and then grabbed her hand and hurried down the sidewalk toward home.

It wasn't until they got home that Caroline asked, "Mama, who was that man?"

"My old hockey coach," she said. "A little older, but same blazer, same bowler hat. I'd recognize him anywhere."

"Why were you scared of him?"

"Well, I wasn't scared. It was just … well, seeing him brought back some memories. A bad one."

"Your leg?"

Mrs. Panski nodded.

"Will you tell me the story now, Mama?"

It was the popping sound she'd never forget. The pain came later. When the injury happened, it was the sound that stunned her.

The girl from the other team couldn't stop herself. Eloise knew that, though she did recall being furious, thinking that perhaps if that woman had more skill on the ice she could have avoided the crash. She remembered the woman as more than a little clumsy, a huge woman who lumbered up and down the ice, whose main purpose was to clear out Spitfire players, to elicit whoops of delight from the crowd when she barreled at top speed into another girl, sending her sprawling and sliding across the ice. It was all spectacle. Eloise knew that. To sell tickets, you needed to give the fans what they wanted. And the guys who came to the games—most of them anyway—just wanted to drink some beer and watch women crash into one another.

But there were other players, women like Eloise, who took pride in their play, who practiced, who tried to win and to win with style and do honor to the sport, playing hockey the way it should have been played.

When that colossus came barreling toward the goal, one of the Spitfire defenders tried to mix her up, clipping her just at her left shoulder. This sent the madwoman spinning on one skate and when she recovered her balance, it was too late. Eloise had come off her line to scoop up the puck and the woman crashed right into her, sending her against the immovable metal goal post and, pop, the leg came out of its socket, the tendons and cartilage twisted and strained and torn.

The pain—and it was terrible—only escalated in the days to come. Her leg swelled up and she spent three days in the hospital and then another two weeks in bed at home, and then six more weeks on crutches. Her playing days were over.

At first, it hit her hard. She mourned for what she had lost. But the season was over in any case and the faint dreams she had of playing the following year managed to dissipate in the happy news of her pregnancy.

Once her daughter came, she didn't think too much of hockey. There were more important things at home. There was her husband to attend to, and she loved him. He was a good and decent man, and he adored her. He proved an excellent father, too—he loved nothing more than taking his baby girl in his arms and spinning her through the air, eliciting spasmodic giggles of delight. Once, when she vomited on him as he spun her around, he didn't even blink. Not even then. He simply placed her down, cleaned himself up, and then started all over again, only slightly less rambunctiously.

So delighted was he with this child, they were soon at work on another. Though it proved more difficult than they anticipated, they kept at it until Sam was born. In the midst of all this, who had time to pine for hockey? Besides, by Sam's second birthday, the women's hockey league had folded.

But still, in certain moments, she couldn't help but allow the memories—the good ones—to sweep over her. There was nothing like the exhilaration of being out there on the ice.

Mrs. Panski looked at her daughter. "So, that's the story. At long last, you know everything."

"I guess it's hard to talk about."

"Yes, it is."

"I'm sorry."

"What do you have to be sorry about?"

"I'm sorry you got injured. And I'm sorry that having me meant you couldn't play anymore, even if your leg healed."

Mrs. Panski smiled a sad smile and put her arms around Caroline. She kissed the top of her daughter's head. "Sweetheart, I told you. I wouldn't trade a trillion games of hockey for you. And if I had it all to do again, I wouldn't change a thing. Not if it meant I got you and Sam. You understand?"

Caroline nodded. "I would have loved to have seen you play, though. I bet you were great."

Mrs. Panski laughed. "I guess I was pretty good."

"I'm sad, Mama."

"I know, sweetheart."

"I'm sad for all the things I never got to see or do, and all the things I never will. And I'm sad about Beautiful and Dad and … just everything."

Mrs. Panski pulled her daughter close and stroked her hair, but Caroline got up and, shoulders hunched, walked up the stairs and into her room, where she closed the door, leaving her mother to navigate her own sadness.

15

CAROLINE SAT ON HER bed. No book, no nothing. Just sat and stared, a sad girl who appeared as if she had lost everything important to her.

After a soft knock on Caroline's bedroom door, Mrs. Panski entered. "Sweetheart? What are you doing?"

"Nothing."

Mrs. Panski started picking up clothes from the floor. "I know things are tough right now." Mrs. Panski continued putting things away, distractedly cleaning up. "There are times in our lives when we are tried. And tried good. Some people fold under the pressure. Others find a way to keep going." She folded a shirt and placed it on Caroline's dresser. "I don't know which category I fall in." Mrs. Panksi stopped what she was doing and looked directly at Caroline. "But I do know which category you fall in. Caroline, look at me."

Caroline did as instructed.

"You are one of the strongest people I know."

One tear fell from Caroline's eye, weaving a path down her cheek. She quickly wiped it away.

"I've sent Sam to the Knudsens. Grab your skates. I want you to come with me."

Caroline climbed off her bed. She started her way out of the room, but Mrs. Panski halted her progress. Clutching her elbow, she leveled a steady gaze at her daughter. "There's a reason I gave them to you, those skates. It scares me to no end. The idea you might end up like me. With this bum leg."

"I won't, Mama. I promise."

"The world doesn't work that way, sweetheart. Some things can't be avoided. But I can't just sit around here watching you be miserable. I can't give you my blessing to play hockey either. But if going out to the ice every now and again with your old mother—"

"You're not old."

"Well. If going out there from time to time and shooting some pucks, if that will put a smile on your face, well, who am I to not allow that, huh?"

Caroline smiled and hugged her mom.

Caroline and Mrs. Panski walked down the street, skates draped over their respective shoulders. Mrs. Panski also carried a large duffel, two hockey sticks poking out the back. Caroline was curious, but she didn't ask where this stuff came from. She was afraid any inquiries would spoil the mood.

When they arrived at the pond, Caroline sat on the ground and put on her skates. Mrs. Panski rifled through the duffel, pulling out all manner of equipment, though it was difficult to tell what it all was.

Caroline finished and stepped out onto the ice. Mrs. Panski removed her jacket, revealing that she was wearing her Spitfires goalie jersey. She dug in the pile of equipment she'd removed from the duffel: goalie gear—mask, glove, big leg and arm pads. She strapped it all on and then headed out onto the ice.

Mrs. Panski's limp was still visible, but being on the ice seemed to have the effect of ironing out the kinks. Her movements certainly couldn't be called graceful, but there was a definite fluidity to them. Her mother ran through some odd dance like a ritual or something: banging on her arm pads, tugging on her mask, skating little choppy steps side to side. Finally, she stopped. She set herself up in front of the netting, dropped a puck onto the ice, and whipped it toward Caroline.

"Show me what you've got, kid."

Caroline collected the puck and started toward goal. It was hard-charging, legs churning, building speed as she bore down on her mother.

Mrs. Panski got herself into position, arms and legs folded inward, cutting off angles and entry points. Caroline continued her charge. She made long looping strides, crossing up the puck, handling the stick masterfully. The puck took a few bumps and skids across the rough surface, but Caroline handled each in turn, never losing control. Around fifteen yards out, she wound back, skated another few yards, and then fired. The puck came zipping through the air toward goal at incredible velocity, a perfect saucer flight, the rubber spinning as beautifully and tightly as the grandest football spiral until *snap!* Mrs. Panski's oversized glove snagged it right out of the air.

Mrs. Panski paused a moment, smiling—it seemed a flood of good memories was coming over her—and then dropped the puck onto the ice. She swept it toward Caroline, who also smiled, clearly impressed.

"You'll have to do better than that."

"I'm not sure I can."

"I'm guessing there isn't anything you can't do if you set your mind to it."

Caroline collected the puck, did the same dance, lined up, fired, and—snap! Same result. Mrs. Panski was clearly in a zone. And she was clearly loving it.

Caroline tried a new tack. She charged hard, lined up to fire, but then put her stick back on the ice and executed a deft little deke as Mrs. Panski stretched toward her. Caroline skipped by her, making a wide arc, and then cut back sharply toward goal, poking the puck behind her laid out mother.

Caroline raised her arms in triumph. Mrs. Panski, despite the obvious sharp registers of pain in her leg, banged on the ice in celebration.

Smiling, laughing—the first time in quite some time—Mrs. Panski and Caroline headed home, both of them bright and flashing from the recent exertion on the ice. But as they got close, Mrs. Panski slowed a bit, the smile fading from her face.

"Mama?" Caroline asked.

Mrs. Panski stopped, maybe a hundred feet from the front stoop.

"Mama? What is it?" Caroline asked.

Still, Mrs. Panski didn't answer. She just kept staring at their house. Caroline looked, too and saw two men there. They were both wearing army uniforms. At first, a jolt of jumbled adrenalin shot through Caroline, for when she saw the uniforms she immediately thought of her father and the next logical leap—that he had returned home—wasn't far behind. But after the first quick glance, she could see neither man was her father. No, these were two strangers who had knocked and were standing there. They knocked again, and when no one answered, they had a short conversation with one another—nothing Caroline could hear—and then started down the stoop.

When they saw Caroline and Mrs. Panski standing on the sidewalk, they made their way over. Mrs. Panski took a step back—barely perceptible, but there nonetheless—as one of the men got close and said, "Mrs. Eloise Panski?" The men seemed unfazed by her hockey getup, as she was still wearing her arm pads, and her mask rested on top of her head, held on by the chinstrap.

"Mrs. Eloise Panski?" the man repeated. The other man stepped close, too. Caroline could see that they both had kind, soft eyes. And they both looked at her with faint smiles. But their eyes were sad and tired, too, and Caroline could see that they held some terrible truth.

Mrs. Panski swallowed hard, stiffened. "That's me."

The men removed the hats from their heads and held them between their fingers—wringing them, balling them up in one direction, releasing, and then balling them up again in the other direction.

"Wife of a Mr. David Panksi, 26th Antiaircraft Artillery Battalion?"

"No."

"No?"

"No!! No, no, no."

The army men managed to catch Mrs. Panski as she crumpled to the sidewalk.

"Mama!" Caroline cried out. She took in the scene, seeing her mother passed out on the sidewalk, the two men trying to revive her. One of them looked up at Caroline. "Sweetheart, can you run inside and get a glass of water?"

Caroline didn't register this request. Instead, she watched as Miss London, their neighbor, came bolting out of her house, running in her housedress toward the scene, running with her hands in the air and her large bosom swaying back and forth.

Caroline stood on the sidewalk, looking at her mother, at Miss London, at the men, and feeling utterly lost in the world.

Miss London caught up to them and wrapped her arms around her, pulling Caroline away from the scene. Instinctively, Caroline twisted away. Then, without knowing how or why, she took off, passing the two old men, still out on the steps chatting about football or hockey or war or whatever, who waved at her as she ran.

Caroline raced through the streets at a full sprint, trying to outrun what she knew was waiting for her back home. She took to the blind alleys, blind now herself with confusion, fear, rage. She skidded to a cross street, sprinted across it without registering the loud honks of the cars swerving to avoid her, and then stopped in front of a house she didn't recognize. She saw it, but she didn't see it. She couldn't register a thing, her thoughts just a jumble in her brain. Then she took off again, trying to run to something, some understanding of something. And then, without even realizing she'd done so, she found herself at the pond. It had been the sight of her last happy moment, so why not go there?

But it didn't help. There was no getting around it. Her daddy was dead. He would never come back home. She would never see him again. She fell to her knees and sobbed.

16

THE FUNERAL WAS HELD in Greenmount Cemetery. She'd been to Greenmount once before. Well, sort of. She and her father had been walking along Oliver Street, away from Penn Station, and turned onto Greenmount Avenue. She couldn't even recall why they were there or what they were doing. In actual crow-fly distance, it wasn't very far from their home, but it was up north past Little Italy, Jonestown, and Oldtown, even beyond Johnston Square and Brentwood, up where Joseph lived. In short, Greenmount West was just not a place they went. But Caroline could remember walking past the cemetery—the great imposing wrought iron gates tucked inside the crenellated stone entrance—and her daddy telling her that eight Baltimore mayors and eight Maryland governors were buried there. Sixteen Civil War generals. Johns Hopkins and Enoch Pratt. Both Walters—Henry and William. The poet Sidney Lanier. Elizabeth Patterson, Napoleon's sister-in-law "Married Napoleon's brother Jerome," her daddy said. Caroline made a face. "It's true," he said. "Lots of others, too. Arunah Abell, the founder of the *Sun* papers. John Wilkes Booth. He's buried there. A whole mess of famous people."

Caroline had tugged on her daddy's sleeve, hurrying the walk. Cemeteries gave her the creeps. He picked up on his daughter's trepidation, for he leaned in close—she could smell his aftershave—and told her that old dumb joke, "C'mon kid, people are dying to get in there."

"Daddy," she said, not laughing, until he poked his fingers into her ribs and she squealed with delight and it didn't matter that they were at a cemetery. She'd had her dad all to herself that day, and there was nothing better than that. Nothing in the whole wide world.

But now she was back at the cemetery for his funeral, and there was no laughter. No more having him to herself. He belonged to everyone now. Everyone and no one. And yet she remained steely somehow, taking it all in, revealing an inner strength well beyond her years. It was as if she'd decided to take the role of family rock when neither Sam nor her mother appeared capable of it.

The funeral was, of course, a dismal affair full of women in black, stoic military men, a somber priest. Mrs. Panski wore all black, too, with a black veil covering her face. Despite the veil hiding her face, the grief and tears and utter devastation came through anyway. Sam was a mess, also, wiping away tears, his face swollen and red.

"We say 'goodbye,' but let us examine the word," the priest said. "'Good-bye. Let us break it up. It means, God be with ye. Those of us who know our French, our Spanish, we look at how those people take leave of one another: 'Adieu,' with God. 'Adios,' be with God. It is the same for us, in our language. David Panski is with God and that means we will see him again."

The tide inside her broke then, mostly because Caroline didn't believe the priest's words and could take no comfort from them. So she ran off, found a huge oak tree to shield herself, and wept for her father, dried leaves clinging to her stockinged knees until several family friends pulled her up and away. Away from the tree. Away from the cemetery. Away from the cold hard place where her Daddy was now and would be forever more.

A week later, Caroline approached school with her books in her arms. She walked with her eyes diverted, aware of the transformation. Many of the other students stared and whispered as she passed. It was clear that word about her dad had gotten around and that she had become an object of supreme fascination.

In class, the students were silent. None of them spoke to her, none of them knew what to say. It was as if Caroline was some strange creature no one knew how to approach safely so everyone just kept their distance. Undeterred, Miss Bloom read a lesson about the Civil War.

"General Benjamin Butler's troops trained their guns on the good citizens of Baltimore from atop Federal Hill—"

Caroline raised her hand.

"Yes, Caroline?"

"I need to use the restroom."

"You may be excused."

Caroline got up and left, the other students watching her every move. Miss Bloom couldn't take her eyes off her, either. Eggshells, for sure.

Once out in the hallway, Caroline ran down the hall until she found a far-off and forlorn looking niche. She leaned against a cinder block wall, slid to the floor, and cried.

She had demanded to come to school, tired of just sitting at home, wearing black, dealing with neighbors and their heaping trays of food, their offers of help when they couldn't really do anything anyway, at least not do the one thing they all wanted and needed. They couldn't bring him back. No one could bring him back alive and well so they could be a whole family again. She was sick of it.

Back in the classroom, Miss Bloom stopped reading, looked at the clock, and glanced at Caroline's empty chair. It had been awhile, at least six or seven minutes. Then she resumed reading. "Executions of Confederate soldiers took place in the courtyard of General Butler's temporary residence on Hamburg Street . . ."

Caroline had by then begun to compose herself. She suddenly became aware of someone approaching and so straightened up, wiping away the last of the tears from her face.

When she looked up, she saw Joseph standing in front of her.

"Hi," he said.

"Hi."

Joseph scratched his arm, the back of his neck. "Are you okay?" he asked, finally.

Caroline nodded.

"You're missing the lesson on The War Between the States."

"That's okay."

"Your daddy died?"

Caroline nodded.

"My daddy died, too."

"In Korea?"

Joseph shook his head. "South Carolina."

"I'm sorry."

Joseph nodded. "You need help getting up?"

"No." Caroline got up and smoothed her skirt. They walked down the hall together, back toward their classroom.

"I had fun that day. You know, when you showed me the ice and all," Joseph said.

"Yeah, me too. How did you get out of class?" Caroline asked.

"Just walked out."

"Aren't you going to get in trouble?"

Joseph shrugged. "I don't care."

"I don't want you to be in trouble on my account."

"We're friends. Sometimes friends get in trouble to help each other."

Caroline nodded and they continued their walk in silence.

Joseph stooped down, picked up a piece of crumpled paper off the floor, carried it with him as they walked, and then deposited it in a hallway trash can.

They came near their classroom door, but Caroline hesitated just before she got there. When she stopped, Joseph, who had been walking just a few steps behind her, stopped, too. He made a noise, a short grunt that Caroline assumed was going to form into a question about whether she was okay. But he got no further than that grunt because Caroline turned around and threw her arms around him, hugging him tightly, stifling sobs.

At first he just stood there. But she kept hugging him, holding on as tightly as she could. Slowly, reluctantly, he raised his hands and hugged her back, allowing her to do whatever it was she needed to do to get it all out.

She didn't make any noises during this long hug, burying her face into Joseph's shoulder. So it wasn't that which drew Beatrice into the hall. It was the fact that more than ten minutes had elapsed between the time Caroline left and when Miss Bloom, now concerned, told Beatrice to go look for her, to check the bathrooms, to see if she was okay. Beatrice, of course, didn't have to go very far. As soon as she opened the door, she saw them. She let out a groan of disgust.

Joseph heard her and dropped his hands immediately. Either Caroline didn't hear, or she didn't care, because she just kept on holding on. If she had extricated herself and turned around, she would have seen Beatrice glaring at them, would have seen the malevolent look in her eye, a look that spoke of real trouble.

Caroline sat on her bed, a book propped on her chest. But she wasn't reading. Instead, she was staring at the ceiling. In the background, she heard her mother call her to supper. But it seemed so far away, she didn't react.

"Caroline!"

Now it registered. The book slid off her chest as she got up. "Coming," she said. But Mrs. Panski didn't hear her.

When Caroline took her place at the table, Mrs. Panski stared at her.

"What?"

"When I call you, I expect to be answered."

"I did answer."

"And I expect to not be lied to. Now, let's say prayers."

Sam mumbled his, Mrs. Panski was barely more audible. Caroline was completely silent.

"Young lady?"

"What?"

"You're too big for prayers now?"

"I don't believe in God," she said, but even she was stunned by the declaration. It felt more for effect than from any real conviction. Still, it came from deep inside, and it had some truth to it. At least in the moment, it was true.

Sam stared at his sister, a mix of awe and shock.

"I'm sorry. What did you just say?"

"I said—"

"I am not deaf and I know perfectly well what you said. The good Lord is the reason we have this food in front of us, and this roof over our heads, and the reason you have the clothes you wear and—"

Braying through a veil of tears, Caroline shouted, "I don't want any of that. You can have all of that. I want my daddy, and my daddy is dead, and God took him away and so I don't believe in him."

"*Caroline!*"

"And you tell me I can't play hockey and I can't be friends with Joseph either. So I don't believe in anything!"

Caroline ran up the stairs. Sam and Mrs. Panski just sat at the table not moving, even after Caroline's bedroom door slammed shut. Finally, Mrs. Panski slowly rose and wordlessly cleared the dishes.

17

CAROLINE WAS HEADING home after school when she heard Beatrice call out to her.

Caroline stopped on the sidewalk, allowing Beatrice to run up.

"Going home?" she asked, catching her breath.

"I have to watch Sam this afternoon."

"Oh, okay, see you."

Beatrice beamed. It was a smile that Caroline had seen before, one that Beatrice turned on in only two circumstances, namely when she sought to use her charms to disentangle herself from some particularly sticky situation, such as the time she and Caroline and Alma had been caught poaching Easter eggs from the lawn of a neighbor who had hidden them in anticipation of a forthcoming hunt. "Hi, Mrs. Twardowicz," Beatrice smiled, three eggs cradled in the long hem of her shirt. "We were just putting these in better hiding spots. I know your back hurts when you bend over, so we'll put them under the bushes for you. The kids will have a much better time hunting if they weren't in such obvious spots, you know."

"Yes, it'll take them longer to find the eggs," Alma put in.

"And that means more time hunting, which is what everyone wants," said Beatrice. "Isn't that right, Caroline?"

Caroline nodded, angry that Beatrice had a habit of always dragging her into whatever mess she had gotten herself into. But angry at herself even more for being unable to resist her. And then Caroline watched as Beatrice laid on the bright smile again, adding with fake compliments, "Mrs. Twardowicz, I do think, without question, your roses are the finest in the neighborhood."

It was only in the last year or so, as Beatrice had finally and completely lost the chubbiness in her cheeks that had defined her as a little girl, did some of the adults seem to wise up to her manipulations.

And then there was the other thing. Beatrice was a good friend to Caroline, had been for years, but she could be downright mean. And when she was scheming something Caroline might think sinister—capturing a cat so that her brother could shave it, for example—she'd get that smile. Caroline saw it as a wicked thing, hardly discernible from the flattering smile but in one respect: the glint in her eyes died. Beatrice possessed lovely green eyes that always seemed to have a little extra layer of moisture in them, giving her the cherubic look of a kid on the edge of crying. But when she got to scheming something particularly nasty, that wetness left her, as if her very soul had dried up and shriveled.

Caroline saw it now, there on the edge of the steps to school, and she wanted none of it.

So she muttered a "goodbye" and hurried on, not looking back.

Alma and Genevieve joined Beatrice on the sidewalk.

"She still sad?" Genevieve asked, seeing Caroline walking home.

"I think she's gone too far," Beatrice said.

"Her father died, Beatrice. Give her a break," Alma said.

"It must be a dreadful time for her."

"I'm sympathetic to that," Beatrice said. "But to run into the arms of a Negro isn't going to help her. I'm sure it will only make things worse. Much worse. Why invite more trouble on yourself?"

"I'm not certain it's really our business," Genevieve said.

"We're her best friends," Beatrice responded. "If it's not our business, whose is it?"

Alma shrugged. "I guess."

"In fact, it's our duty to help her—even if she acts like we're the worst people in the world," Beatrice said.

Genevieve and Alma didn't say anything. They just stole a quick glance at each other, the way they did when Beatrice got a head of steam about something and the two of them—or, in what felt like the old days, the three of them, including Caroline—were powerless to stop her. They still said nothing, even as Beatrice turned and walked away from them, heading back into school.

As Joseph walked through the hallway toward the front doors, he turned a corner and there stood Beatrice.

"Hi," she said.

Joseph didn't react.

"I'm Beatrice. We're in Miss Bloom's class together."

"I know who you are."

"You and Caroline seem to be very close."

Joseph shrugged. On edge, he looked back and forth and from side to side.

"You don't have anything to be scared about."

"I'm not scared."

"I just want to be friends with you, like Caroline. In fact, she's looking for you. She told me to tell you to meet her at the playground."

"Why didn't she just tell me herself?"

"You know Caroline. I mean, I think she's wonderful, but she likes rules. And Miss Bloom is strict about talking in class. Besides, when Miss Bloom saw you two in the hallway, well, I think Caroline thought that she was already in enough trouble."

Beatrice paused, she seemed unsure of her next move. This unnerved Joseph even more.

"Well, okay then. Goodbye." Beatrice held out her hand to shake, then retracted it, then put it out again, tentatively. But Joseph wasn't taking her hand in any case. He just stood there, unmoving.

"Well okay then," Beatrice repeated, pulling her hand away again, seemingly not upset or offended by Joseph's rejection of it, or of her. She went to leave, but then called over her shoulder. "See you at the playground. Don't forget."

Outside, Joseph walked in the opposite direction of the playground.

Beatrice turned and spotted him walking away. She took off in a trot and caught up with him. "Hey, I thought you were meeting Caroline. Didn't I tell you that you need to go to the playground, silly?"

Joseph said nothing.

"She told me she was expecting you at the playground. You don't want to disappoint her, do you? I know she'd be disappointed if she showed up and you weren't there."

"I need to get home now," Joseph said. He squinted into the sun and held his hand up to shield his eyes. "And I don't want any trouble."

"What trouble? You'd think we were all commies or something."

Just then, Alan and two other boys from the hockey rink appeared from around the corner of the school. They walked right up to Joseph.

"Aren't you supposed to be at the playground to see your little white girlfriend?" Alan asked.

"She's not my girlfriend."

"You sure right she ain't, nigger," one of the other boys said. "You don't even belong here."

Joseph glared, anger flashing across his face. His jaw set. He was more than ready for a rumble. But it was three against one. He looked at Beatrice, who gave him a wicked grin.

Joseph took off running and the three boys pursued.

They looked like wolves as they ran. Joseph glanced over his shoulder to watch them. They were not getting any closer, and, in fact, on two occasions, they stumbled over each other, almost spilling to the ground in their zeal to catch him. At one point, Joseph almost laughed, a combination of nervous titters and the fact that they just looked so stupid. They had little chance of catching him. He hadn't even hit second gear yet, saving it for the moment they might close in. But one of the three had already fallen far behind and when Joseph next looked back, he could see the overweight kid had stopped, bent over with his hands on his knees and sucking breath. Not long after, a second one tripped. When Joseph stole a glance, he saw the kid lying on the ground holding his knee, a tear in his pants. But Alan still pursued.

Down the street, through an alley, past the frozen pond.

Joseph was willing to draw him in further, lead him toward his own neighborhood. Once he could be sure it was just the two of them left, Joseph would stop, allow Alan to catch up, and then punch him square in the nose. Just one or two more blocks. But then Joseph turned into a dead end. As he changed course, he saw Alan coming into the blind alley. He and Joseph just stopped, staring at one another, catching their breath. And then, a moment later, the other two boys arrived.

There was another moment of pause. Joseph watched the three boys; they watched him. And then it started as if by some sort of silent decree, the three white boys went at him simultaneously.

Joseph fought back, landing a few punches, but was soon overwhelmed. And soon enough, the white boys beat the tar out of him, slashing at him with fists and shoes and stopping only when Alan told them to, but not before he landed two or three more rapid fire punches on the back of Joseph's head. Joseph wrapped his arms over his head, but the damage was done.

Satisfied, the boys started to move away, chests heaving, sweat dripping.

"Maybe Caroline can come bandage up her little nigger friend," Alan spit.

The boys left Joseph, bloodied and bruised, in the alley.

He lay there a long time, occasionally straightening his legs and then pulling them up again against his chest. He had trouble drawing a full breath and when he tried, a sharp stab of pain flashed through his ribs.

Eventually, he got himself up and limped his way home, some twenty blocks. Each step brought on more painful stabs of air, more reminders of his place in this world. But he wouldn't cry. Nuh-uh. Never, not in a million years. He'd take his lumps. He'd known they'd come someday. This was something all little back boys knew. It was one of the few things he could remember his Daddy sitting him down and telling him. Mostly, the old man just grunted his way through life. But that one time, he took Joseph out on the porch and looked him in the eye and said, straight as an arrow, "You stay out of trouble. There'll be times you'll want to scream and thrash and tell those ignorant crackers what's up. But you hold your tongue, boy. If you know what's good for you, you hold your tongue. No matter if it ain't even true. You keep yourself out of the situation in the first place. They's just looking for you to slip up. Just looking for it. You keep your head down and you hold your tongue. Make it through, son. Just make it through."

The last block before home, he passed three men sitting out on their stoops playing the dozens. "Your mama so fat, she . . ." and "Your old lady so dumb, she . . ." But they stopped jabbing each other when they saw Joseph pass. They shook their heads. But Joseph kept walking. None of them stopped him, or asked what had happened.

They knew all too well.

18

THE STUDENTS IN Miss Bloom's class were writing in their tablets while Miss Bloom sat at her desk grading.

Caroline looked over toward Joseph's empty desk. He wasn't in school. Hadn't been all day. She got back to her work.

"Psssst." It was Alma. Caroline looked over.

"Did you hear?" Alma whispered.

Caroline shook her head.

"Joseph was beaten up yesterday."

"What—? By who?"

Miss Bloom glanced up from her work. "Caroline Panski, is there a problem?"

"No, ma'am."

Caroline and Alma got back to their work. But after another few moments, Alma turned back to Caroline and whispered. "It was pretty bad."

Caroline wanted to scream, wanted to do something, *anything*, but there was nothing she could do stuck in the classroom.

Alma tapped her foot on the ground to get Caroline's attention again. "Don't worry. He's not dead, though."

Just hearing the word was enough for Caroline. She scrambled out of her desk and burst out of the classroom, heels clacking down the hallway until she pushed right out of the front door of the school. This time, unlike every other day when she headed left for home, she turned right, toward the part of Baltimore where she knew Joseph lived, somewhere deep over the color line, but unsure where. No matter—she headed that way anyway.

It wasn't long before the flavor of the neighborhoods changed. There were the same old rowhomes and the same old stoops she found in her neighborhood. But there was more garbage collected along the curbs, more cracks in the sidewalk, more dormant weeds pushing up through the cement. But she continued, even as the scenery got worse, even in the face of small piles of broken glass lying near the curbs, even past houses with stoops that were not only not polished, but full of chips and scrapes and scuffs. Joseph's house couldn't have been too much further ahead. She began to consider it as something of a refuge. She needed only to reach his house. But how she'd find it, she had no idea.

She turned onto Eager Street heading toward Preston, where Joseph had told her he lived, and saw three men sitting on their stoop talking and laughing. As Caroline approached, they stopped and stared.

"You a long way from home," one of them said.

"You lost little girl?" asked a second.

"I'm looking for Joseph," she said nervously.

"Joe Louis? Famous boxer? Ain't from around here."

"Maybe she's looking for Joe Gans."

"No luck in that, either," the third man said. "Less you want to run over Mount Auburn Cemetery and dig him up. It's thataway."

The men laughed, but it was good-natured, a clear attempt to defuse what could have been a potentially explosive situation. "What you want with these old fighters anyway?" they continued, the rag still full on.

Undeterred, Caroline told them: "I'm looking for Joseph Wilson. Colored boy. Lives around here somewhere."

"Lots of colored boys live around here, don't you know."

"And I suspect quite a few of them named Joe Wilson. Pretty common name."

"He goes to the white school south of here," Caroline explained.

One of the men turned to another and said, "Say, isn't that Mavis's boy? The one integrating the school down Patterson Park?"

"Walked through here all beaten up yesterday?"

"That's him," Caroline said.

"If it is, you in luck little lady. Mavis lives just around this corner here, on Wolfe. 1104, I believe it is."

"Thank you, sir."

"Good luck to you."

Caroline started to walk away.

"Say, you got something stuck behind your ear there," one of the men said.

"What?"

"Can't hear me cause you got something stuck behind your ear. Come here."

Caroline went and stood before him. The man reached out behind her head and slowly, steadily pretended to be extracting something good and jammed. Then, with a quick jerk, he ripped his hand from behind her head, opened his palm, and revealed a shiny copper penny. "Here you go," he said, handing it to her. "Now you should be able to hear better."

Caroline smiled and deposited the penny in her pocket.

"Say, what you want with this Joe Wilson anyway?" the man asked.

Caroline looked him square in the face and said, "He's my friend."

1104 Wolfe Street was a fine enough place, solidly built, with multi-colored bricks lain one atop the other with extraordinary precision and with an attractive plaster decoration— some kind of tree branch—just above the lintel. And yet there was a certain shabbiness to Caroline's eye, a sense of neglect just at the outer edges of this house, with its collection of curbside litter, its stray Coke and beer bottles, its scuffed and unclean stoop. This whole block was teetering on some edge, a long slide into despair. Even the weather seemed harsher here, and for the first time, Caroline became aware of being cold.

She walked up to the front door, hesitated and then sucked in her resolve. She knocked and then jumped back at the response: ferocious barking coming from inside.

There was a struggle to open the door, but when it swung open, it revealed a tall, thin woman in a floral housedress with her gray hair pulled back on her head. She bellowed to someone inside, "Take the dog to the back room!" Then, she turned and addressed Caroline in a curt voice. "Can I help you?"

"Is this where Joseph Wilson lives?"

"And who wants to know?" Her voice was laced with impatience, even accusation.

"Caroline Panski."

Caroline knew this must be Granny. She folded her arms across her chest and stared, serious daggers in her eyes. Clearly she was not someone to fool with.

Caroline swallowed. "Is Joseph home?" she ventured.

"And where else do you expect him to be?"

"He wasn't in school today."

"He wasn't in school today because some boys beat him up—could be your brothers by the looks of you. Three boys against one of him."

"I came to see if he's okay."

"He'll be okay."

"Will he be back in school?"

There was movement behind Granny and she became distracted.

"Granny, who's there?"

Caroline recognized Joseph's voice.

"Get back in there and lay down," Granny demanded.

"It's me," Caroline said.

The door opened, revealing Joseph. There was a bandage across his head, and one eye was black and puffy. He had a cut across his lower lip and one arm in a sling. Granny stepped back, allowing Caroline full view of this pathetic spectacle and then fixed her with a mile long stare, as if this was Caroline's doing.

"What happened?"

"As if you don't know."

"What? I don't know. What do you mean?"

"It was your friends did this to me."

"No, Joseph. That's not true."

"I don't want to see you again."

Joseph looked to Granny for some kind

of confirmation, which she gave by way of a firm nod before scooting Joseph back inside. When he was in, she turned to Caroline.

"You heard the boy. Now I suggest you get yourself back to your neighborhood where you belong."

The door slammed hard, a final exclamation point. Then, just as quickly, the door opened again. "Little lady," Granny called.

Caroline, full of renewed hope, answered, "Yes?"

"Here." She tossed Caroline's scarf and it fell to the ground as the door slammed shut.

She started to walk away when the door opened again. This time, it was Joseph.

"You have to believe me," Caroline said. "I swear I didn't know a thing about it. They're not even my friends. I don't think I even have friends anymore."

"I know it wasn't you," Joseph said. "I had to say that because of Granny."

"I missed you today. You're coming back to school, aren't you?"

Joseph shook his head.

"But you have to."

"They don't want me there."

"Well, they don't want me either."

"But they don't aim to kill you. I seen how this works. My daddy—"

"My daddy is dead, too, you know. You're not the only one in the world with a dead daddy."

"You don't understand. You don't know anything about it."

"I know that you can't leave."

"Why not?"

"Because you're all I've got left. I gave up my friends for you. My dad is dead. I don't have hockey. My mom is hardly there anymore. She's there, but she's not there. It's just you, Joseph. You're all that's left."

Joseph stared down the cold street, looking pathetic in his bandages. "I'm sorry, Caroline," he said. "I'm going to a different school. A Negro school."

Caroline felt a deep anger burning inside

her. She was alone in the world and Joseph was the only one who could understand her. "I thought you were braver than that," she said.

Joseph shook his head. "I'm plenty brave. Goodbye, Caroline," he said.

Dejected, she walked away, just as a light snow began to fall. Behind her, Joseph bent and picked up her scarf. He started to call out for her, but her name got caught in his throat. Besides, by this point, she had already turned a corner and was gone.

As Caroline walked toward home, she passed the alley that led to the frozen pond. She heard the shouts of the boys, deep into a game. She turned around and marched straight down the alley and emerged onto the ice.

She stood there a minute, completely numb to the world, numb to everything, unaware of what she was going to do. Until one of the creeps hurled some stupid insult at her. Again. And that was that. Enough was enough.

She marched up to the boy, the kid whose stick she snatched last time around. This time he wisely handed it to her, no questions asked. She grabbed it and stepped out onto the ice. She wore regular shoes, so she was at a severe disadvantage. But she was a player possessed, stealing the puck from one of the boys and racing toward goal. Her teammates called for the puck, banging the ice to alert her to their positions. But she ignored all of them. When a defender approached, she took her stick and cracked him across the kneecaps. He crumpled in a pained heap. She got close to goal and shot. This time the goalie made the save.

Caroline turned around to see Alan skating full speed toward her, a repeat of when she scored and he laid her out. But this time she raised her stick and slammed it right across his mouth. He went sprawling, his mouth sprinkling the ice with blood. One tooth skittered across the ice. Caroline threw down her stick and jumped on top of Alan, walloping his face with her hands, a combination of slaps and punches, fighting against the universe, taking out all of her fury toward an unfair world, until several of the other boys lifted her off and held her back. She struggled for a few moments before wrestling free and taking off back across the ice and through the alley, leaving a dozen stunned boys to watch Alan writhe on the ice.

She walked faster now, impervious to the cold. She skirted the edges of her own neighborhood and walked all the way past Highlandtown, along North Highland Street, past the tall thin brick and Formstone rowhomes. She kept going, picking up Lombard Street and turning south down Haven Street. She walked for an hour, through neighborhoods she didn't recognize and where she knew no one. Baltimore was funny that way, she thought. You only had to go a few blocks in one direction or another and you were in a new world. The houses were different, the people were different, you could hear different languages.

Then, she thought she started to recognize things. But why? Or how? And then it hit her. If she kept going in the same direction, soon enough she'd run out of land. There, not far ahead, was the place where the big ships docked, where she'd seen her daddy off, not even a year earlier. It felt like a whole other life altogether. And that, suddenly, was where she needed to go. No question about it.

A gargantuan ship sat in port, just like the last time she'd been there. But this time it was discharging soldiers, not taking them on board. There was a crowd, too, whole families, waiting with hardly concealed excitement on the pier, looking and straining, hoping to catch the first glimpse of their loved one coming home. Several young children strained at their mother's knees, like dogs pulling on leashes, ready to burst forward and run to their daddies.

And there, coming from a single open

door, one by one, men in drab green uniforms, each of them carrying a huge duffel across his back, emerged onto a gangway and made his way toward the series of ladders and steps that would take him onto land, take him to his waiting family. Twice, she saw men that looked, from her distance, exactly like her own father. His handsome face. His smooth grin. The dark hair, combed neatly under his drab olive hat. She even saw the faint indentation of the dimple in his chin. But each time this happened, the man who looked initially like her father morphed into some other man, a man with a different family, a man who wrapped his arms around some other woman—not Caroline's mother—and some other kids—not her and Sam. And arm in arm they walked off. And there Caroline stood alone.

Each man who came off the final ladder shook the hand of a guy with a thin mustache and slicked back hair, dapper in a dark suit, who Caroline eventually recognized as the mayor of Baltimore. And then it was over. The mayor headed toward a long, black waiting car. The happy families dispersed and made their way toward the freeways of Baltimore, Maryland, the United States of America, back, presumably, to warm meals and happy homes.

But, in fact, it wasn't over. After a few moments, Caroline noticed there were easily a dozen or so other families still standing around. They were all Negro. The same kind of excitement swept over them, too, but they had been somehow invisible just minutes earlier. It was only now, as the dark-skinned men started leaving the ship, that these folks, too, ran toward it, leaping and twirling, and grasping onto their returning heroes. Caroline watched these families, too, not even realizing that long steaks of tears flowed down her cheeks.

19

"A WORLD OF HURT." That's what Sam used to call it, though he joked about it. It was some dumb phrase he'd picked up from his friends at school. "Hey, Caroline," he'd say. "I'm gonna put you in a world of hurt." He'd say this while holding up his pointer finger and thumb, cocking a make believe gun.

"Shut up, Sam," she'd say.

But now she kind of knew what he was talking about, or at least was feeling what she imagined a world of hurt actually felt like. A hollowed out feeling, like her belly was nothing but a big deep hole and what bounced around in there was a mess of butterflies all flapping their wings and making her feel perpetually on the edge of being sick.

She missed her dad. She'd never see him again. It hurt so much to think about it.

And Joseph was gone now, too, transferred to a different school. The one good thing was that Alan was gone also, sent to a military school or something, the rumor went, as discipline for his role in Joseph's beating. But she didn't care about Alan. It was Joseph she missed. It seemed everyone important to her was nothing more than a ghost now, all of them residing in some place she could never hope to get to.

Worse, whenever she caught eyes with Beatrice, her old friend glared at her. Even Genevieve wasn't acting nice, though it seemed to Caroline that she simply didn't know where to turn her allegiances and was uncomfortable with the tension between her old friends, so she did what she always did in situations that made her uncomfortable—she clammed up entirely.

It remained unspoken, but just like Joseph's presence had created and maintained a deep wedge between Caroline and her friends, now his absence did the same.

"Hey, guys ..." Alma started. But when the only response was a snapped, "What?" all she managed was a chastened, "Forget it" before the group of old friends dispersed leaving Alma alone and, presumably, dreaming of television. She wanted an end to it, clearly, but she did not possess the power of reconciliation between her more forceful friends, and so the girls continued in a silent stalemate over something that none of them was capable of naming and none of them tried to resolve.

The same scene repeated itself each day for the rest of the week. In the lunchroom and outside the building before and after school, Alma was literally and figuratively in the middle, between Caroline on one side and Beatrice and the complicit Genevieve on the other, with backs turned in icy silence and no one interested in a thaw or even in trying to understand what it was really all about.

So Caroline walked home from school alone. Most days, that was just fine. It seemed that for most of the kids, accumulating as many friends as possible was the highest form of validation. But Caroline never could see the fuss in it. A few good friends was more than sufficient. And lately it was clear that even her old friends were tiring of her. So be it. The prospect would have horrified her not long ago, but now she felt a certain comfort in solitude. Still, it was no fun to be alone all the time. But she just couldn't be around Beatrice and Genevieve anymore. Alma wasn't bad, but still …

The problem was that Caroline felt like a totally different person now than the person she had been barely six months earlier. It was as if she had aged a whole four or five years. She could get back to her friends when they caught up to her, or when she reverted back to being her old self. Until then, she'd go it alone.

The trolley was a rare treat. True, it cost only five cents, a fare the Panskis could afford from time to time, but there just wasn't any real need. Virtually everything they could want they could get by walking. But Caroline decided she deserved a treat. She knew what she'd find over at the frozen pond—no doubt those creeps would be back. She wanted to get away from them, away from her own neighborhood for a while, from her life, if that was possible.

So she pulled a dime from her piggy bank, grabbed her skates and stick, and took the Number 29 north toward Roland Park. She knew exactly where she wanted to go.

She couldn't remember where she and her dad had been heading when they'd left the house that morning. It seemed so long ago now. It had been like any other morning, but Caroline knew it would turn into something special when her dad tapped her knee well before their stop, stood up, and winked at her. "Come on. Let's get off here."

They'd exited the trolley across from the grand Cathedral on Charles Street and walked a few blocks toward Loyola College, stopping along the way for two lemon Italian ices. It was a blazing hot summer day. "I want to show you something," he said, walking briskly up Charles and turning on Cold Spring. Just before them stood a great hill.

"What's that, Daddy?"

"Come on, I'll race you up." He took off up the hill. Caroline chased after, and soon she caught and then passed him.

He got to the top of the hill and bent over, his hands on his knees, breathing in and out as if he'd just run a marathon. "You're … just … too … fast," he wheezed. "Whew!"

"Stop it, Daddy," she said with a laugh, and then turned to see a lake in the shape of a perfect square with a big flock of geese floating on top. "What is this place?"

"The Guilford Reservoir. Can you imagine that? A neighborhood so fancy it's got its own water supply."

Caroline scrunched up her nose. "But don't the geese poop in it?"

Her father rubbed his knuckles over Caroline's head. "That'll be our little secret, won't it?" He patted the ground and she sat next to him. Below them they could see the rooftops of Guilford, the toniest enclave in the city. Stone and stucco beauties planted like fairy tale castles along curvy streets studded with sycamores and poplars—a place that seemed a million miles from where they lived, and yet was less than a few miles from home. In a distant, fantastical way, it felt like home—or a place one would aspire to call home someday.

"You think you might like to live down there one day?" her father asked. "You and some drop-dead gorgeous guy?" He poked a finger in her ribs.

"It is beautiful," she said, squirming away. "But I can't imagine I'd ever live in a place like this."

"Sweet Caroline, you can do anything you want to do. Of that I am certain."

She remembered that conversation now, and it seemed a cruel one. It bit at her, nibbling at her chest and threatening to spill tears down her cheeks, tears that would not stop if she allowed them to start. So she bit them back and sat on the ground at the reservoir's edge, lacing up her skates. The sky was overcast and gray and a false dawn spread itself all around her in the form of a thick gloom. Tiny plumes of smoke curlicued their way from the chimney tops below her, melding with the atmospheric gray. Single candles lit many of the windows.

This was one of the problems with going to a place like Guilford. Yes, she wanted an escape. But the temporary nature of it was almost too much to bear. Did someone from Caroline's Highlandtown neighborhood ever wind up in a place like this? Did that migration ever really occur? Or did people like Caroline automatically stay in what she had once heard her neighborhood referred to as "blue collar"? It was just one more thing in a seemingly endless list of things that didn't make sense. She knew one of her neighbors, six houses down, had painted his front door and the window trims blue, but what did that have to do with "collars"? Who knew?

Anyway, it didn't much matter; her father was gone now and with him all his dreams for her. Yes, the military provided some survivors' pay, but this was only enough to keep the family afloat. Was it realistic to think that she'd end up anywhere besides where she'd come from?

And yet her thoughts of Highlandtown shamed her, too. It wasn't as if she was embarrassed about where she'd come from. It was a solid place, far better and more secure than neighborhoods like where Joseph lived. Highlandtown had been a major step up for her grandparents, émigrés from Poland and Austria-Hungary who'd settled in Baltimore looking for a new life, free from Old World prejudices, seeking a world where if one simply worked hard enough, rewards awaited. A "meritocracy," her dad called it. It was the first "adult word" she'd ever learned. Sure, it was plenty good enough for them. It was just that her dad pictured her elsewhere, up here, and not down there.

But that was just it, though, wasn't it? When she thought about her grandparents now—she'd only ever met two of them and they both died when she was young—she remembered them only as very old and so hopelessly out of style with their modest clothing and penchant for layering themselves, even in summer, in the drabbest, most unflattering garments.

She remembered her grandmother's chin and the long silver hairs that sprouted there. She'd be ashamed to admit it out loud, but now, after so many years, if she was honest, she'd concede that when her grandmother insisted on a hug, Caroline complied but not without a shudder. And she could remember virtually nothing of her grandfather besides his grotesque nose, bulbous and shaped like a grenade speckled with the blue of burst capillaries.

Yes, they had made sacrifices, and she was glad of it. They had done what they needed to do to make a better life, so what did she owe them now if not to keep moving on up the ladder? Was it fruitless to think she could live in a place like this? Her father thought she could. He thought she could do anything. But could she?

Lacing up her skates, she saw her father in the reflection on the ice. She saw the geese, too, gone now for the season. And she saw Joseph, saw his hopelessness on the ice, the comic way he had of skittering his shoes along the surface as if he was a cartoon character slipping on a strategically placed banana peel. She remembered the feel of his hand—so warm and smooth, the skin on his palm a full two shades lighter than the backside—reaching out to her for help as he struggled to stay on his feet.

She stepped on to the ice and took off full speed across the reservoir. She sprinted back and forth, back and forth, exhausting herself. But it felt good to feel the pain, to suck in the cold wind, to cramp up. It reminded her of real life and while that was the last thing she wanted, it was where she must return and where she'd spend her days, so why not make a friend of the pain? She held her stick across her chest, swept it down low on the ice, reared back, and fired slapshots with invisible pucks at an imaginary net.

She ran through the same routine again, only this time, just as she was about to shoot, her skate caught a divot that sent her sprawling across the surface. She slid to the edge of the ice and crumpled onto the frozen ground.

She did not get up. Instead, she cried— long and hard and with abandon. She wasn't hurt physically. Instead she cried for an injury that penetrated deep inside and that had been begging for release.

When she got home, she took her skates and hockey stick and bundled them down to the cellar. There, she pressed her lips to the Clippers man on her stick, held back more tears, and placed it behind a pile of taped up boxes, out of sight. Like some sort of burial ritual, she took the laces of her skates, wrapped them around the boots, threading them through the open space between sole and blade, and then tucked them inside a box and put them away.

She hardly knew what she was doing as she did it, but it felt to her like the right thing to do, the only thing to do. It was something she couldn't name and something she didn't understand. Something that told her that hockey belonged to a part of her life that was over now, that her need to assert herself in a world that told her she couldn't do things was a losing strategy in the end, that maybe, in some weird way, the universe was punishing her for even trying, for daring to scream, "Yes, I can!" at a world that told her, "No, you can't be anything you want. No, you can't do what you want. No, Miss Caroline Panski. No, you can't."

20

THOUGH THE DAYS AND WEEKS seemed endless, they passed nonetheless. Mother Nature offered up longer days, barely perceptible at first until the sun was still up past 5 p.m. The daffodils bloomed, followed by daisies and tulips. Then the presence of a few solitary buds. The trees burst forth soon after, and all at once it seemed, donning their fuzzy coats in a gorgeous and life-affirming display.

The boaters took to Druid Lake. Kids skipped stones across Lake Montebello. Families picnicked atop Federal Hill. Wash day came and whole families appeared on their front stoops wielding cans of Ajax and scrub brushes until the marble shined. And the hockey pond turned into a soupy mix of rainwater and mud.

Spring continued its lovely march unabated, soon melding into a blazing hot summer that, despite the malaise-inducing heat, was a glorious prospect of long days and endless promises. But soon it became nothing more than heat and boredom.

Caroline was certain she'd read every book in the local library, and it was still only July. Her mother suggested she go to the pool at Druid Hill, but, of course, she wouldn't go. She wouldn't go because she'd have to walk past the "Negro pool" crammed with hundreds of people. Yes, the people using it acted happy enough, but the indignity of it was too much. The pool was one large square—a paltry four feet deep all around and had no diving board. It was barely deep enough to lower yourself under, and if you did, it was so crowded that you'd probably wind up with a knee in the eye.

Yet she'd have to pass the Negro pool to get to the white one, with its snack bar, its tables with umbrellas for shade, its diving board and slide, its deep end, and its happy, privileged families. Of course, the real privileged families were at their private clubs, and there were loads of them, practically overlapping one another all across the broad, manicured spectrum of north central Baltimore.

Druid Hill was no luxury, Caroline knew that. She knew that when she went to the white pool, most of the kids were from families just like hers. But to be within earshot of the Negro pool, to know what the scene was just over the hill was too much. No, she would not go to Druid Hill.

So Caroline sat in her room, passing long hours doing nothing but resisting her mother's requests that she get out, do something. Sam flew out of the door by nine each morning and often didn't return until suppertime. Of course, the activities acceptable for a young boy were essentially without limit. Not so for her, Caroline reminded her mother. "Oh, please, Caroline. You don't believe that for a second," Mrs. Panski responded, and Caroline couldn't even bring herself to argue about it.

"What about your friends?" Mrs. Panski asked.

Caroline did occasionally go over to Alma's, but the last two times she'd gone there, it was terrible. She'd watched silently while Alma and her mother gaped at the television, watching *Strike it Rich* which featured wretched people explaining their tales of woe—a needed surgery or a poor family living in a destitute place— who had to answer a series of questions to win some money. In one episode, the woman answering the question—she was missing a tooth right up front—flubbed a pretty easy one: "What state was George Washington from?" She answered, "California," and lost the $90 she had already accumulated. The audience groaned while Alma and her mother, practically in shock, asked each other how on earth she'd missed that. The host opened up the "Heart Line," a phone line for viewers to call in and donate to the woman and her family. The show gave Caroline a stomachache, and she excused herself. Neither Alma nor her mother noticed her leaving.

And so the summer ground on, molasses-like, toward fall and a return to school. Except this time school was different—it was junior high.

The junior high school was bigger and there were more kids from adjacent neighborhoods, some from merely a few blocks away, but places Caroline had hardly ever ventured and didn't know much about. In contrast, she knew every street and block in her own neighborhood, which she mentally defined as a radius of three or four blocks around her house.

She found that the kids from Patterson Park seemed to carry a chip on their shoulder. In school they moved in packs and were loud and boisterous, as if they had something to prove. Same with the North Canton kids who could be seen huddling in groups in the cafeteria and before and after school. The sprinkle of kids from Brewers Hill, less a residential area than the place where their dads worked in the breweries—Hamms, Gunther's, National Bohemian, Pabst's—seemed primarily to keep to themselves, too, content not to raise any trouble. And of course there were the black kids from Linwood who knew enough, despite their increased numbers, to keep their heads down.

To Caroline's mind, the black kids carried a certain quiet dignity with them. Often, she looked over at them at their table in the cafeteria and wished she could simply go over and sit with them, befriend them, swap pieces of their lunches. But her old friends thought she was weird enough already. Of course, she didn't see or talk to the girls who used to be her closest friends much anymore anyway. Alma hadn't forgotten Caroline's distaste of television, though the two of them did get together occasionally, Genevieve was going to a Catholic school, and while Beatrice went to the same school as Caroline—they were even in the same homeroom—she and Caroline hadn't spoken to one another since Joseph was beaten up.

She learned from a black classmate that Joseph was now attending a church school up in Middle East—just for black kids. One time, on an errand with her mother to see an inexpensive and apparently expert seamstress recommended by a friend, they passed through McElderry and Elwood Park, past the color line at Madison and Biddle. There, Caroline saw a group of black girls and boys spilling from some church doors in matching uniforms—blue slacks and skirts, white button up shirts, blue ties for the boys, blue hair ribbons for the girls—and scanned them all looking for Joseph. But she didn't see him, or at least she couldn't know for sure if she saw him. Through the gauzy bus window, coupled with the speed with which they passed, combined with the fact—embarrassed though she would have been to admit it out loud—that the boys all looked the same to her with their hair cut close on their head, she just couldn't know if he was one of them.

So just like that, he was gone, as if swallowed whole by the city, by the times, by events larger than the both of them put together.

So the school year went on this way—fall to winter, winter to spring, spring to summer—just like it always had. Caroline focused on her school work and did her best to not think too much about the things that used to provide her pleasure and that were no more: her father, hockey, Joseph. She never even went over to the frozen pond during the winter. It was too painful. Her skates and stick remained tucked away in the basement. Going back there, retrieving them, would remind her too much of her father, and so she didn't do it.

Instead, she built imaginary bubbles around herself. Whenever things got too difficult, she closed her eyes and blew out, imagining a force field around her to keep her safe. It worked, most of the time. But she knew what people said about her, that she was quiet and withdrawn, and that she was resigned.

Of course, Caroline wasn't completely without friends. It was easy enough to make new school friends. But that's really all they were—school friends, nothing more. She still saw Alma occasionally, but separate interests turned them into mere acquaintances, girls who had shared good times and memories when they were younger, but who now regarded those earlier years as little more than a prelude to the present.

But, for Caroline, the present held little promise. The Panskis seemed to be living in their own separate worlds. Sam was always busy with school and activities. Her mother was always busy, too. Her mother no longer asked for her help with Sam and rarely even asked what she was up to or reminded her to attend to her studies. Because Caroline was an ace student, schoolwork had never been an issue, and so now that she was in junior high, she was left to her own devices. She could come and go as she pleased, within limits of course.

But what did all this independence get her? Her life was boring. Everything was boring. Boring. Boring. Boring. Boring. Nothing but the same thing, over and over and over again, even in a new school.

21

Mrs. Panski sat on the edge of Caroline's bed. "Don't you have something to do?" she asked.

Caroline shook her head and kept her eyes on her book.

"What about your friends?"

"I don't have any friends, Mama. Not ones I want to see anyway."

"That can't be true. I know things haven't been great with Beatrice and Genevieve and Alma, but—"

"I gave them all up for Joseph. I just wanted to spend time with someone who understood me. His daddy died, too. None of my friends understand."

Mrs. Panski winced and turned away, hiding the tears brimming in her own eyes.

Then, without a word, she got up, left the room, and then returned a moment later.

"Here," she said, handing a piece of paper to Caroline.

"What is it?"

"I saw it posted while I was shopping the other day. Read it."

Caroline unfolded the paper and read while Mrs. Panski left the room again. "Open call. Hockey Club tryouts. Sports Center, North and Calvert, Balto."

Caroline looked it over a few times. She didn't know what it meant.

Mrs. Panski returned, holding Caroline's skates and stick. "It's time," she said.

"Mama—"

"I've watched you mope around this house for over a year now. You need to snap out of it. And this"—she pressed the stick and skates on the bed next to Caroline—"is the only thing I know of that will do the trick. It scares me no end, Caroline. That you'll get hurt. If you do, well, I'm not sure I'll be able to live with myself. But I can't just sit around and allow you to stay miserable forever."

"But—"

"Oh, Caroline, stop. You don't believe in 'but.' You never did and you never will. This past year has been hard, but now it's time to make a change. Do this for me, for your father. Do it for yourself, it doesn't matter. Just don't give up. Because if you do, you'll never forgive yourself. And if you never forgive yourself, I'll never forgive myself. You understand?"

Caroline nodded. She did, indeed, understand. Before, hockey reminded her too much of her dad, which was too painful, so she just couldn't bring herself to play. But now, well, it reminded her of her dad, and so she wanted to do it. It was time.

Many of the city's elite private schools— Gilman, Boys Latin, Loyola Blakefield, among them—fielded hockey teams, and the competition was always fierce. The boys who filled out these teams knew they had to practice hard, and so a flourishing club level existed for just this purpose.

But girls? No way.

But that reality made it even more attractive to Caroline. She was ready for another chance to show the boys what she was made of, to show them she could be just as good as they were. Even better.

When she tried on the skates, they were a bit snug, but they'd do. Thank goodness they were big when her mom gave them to her. All she needed now were pads. She took all the money she'd ever saved—from Christmases, the tooth fairy, odd gifts for occasions she could no longer remember—and turned it all over to Mr. Reider, who owned a sporting goods store on Eastern.

"You're thirty-nine cents short," Mr. Reider said after counting it all out. "What do you need this for anyway?"

"I'm trying out for a hockey club."

Mr. Reider grinned, revealing several missing teeth. The remaining choppers were not only yellowed, but appeared blackened in the middle. Holes? Food? Tobacco? Caroline didn't know, but the sight nearly made her sick. She shuddered and bit back the angry comment bubbling behind her tongue. She started to sweep her money back off the counter.

"Well, hold on now," Mr. Reider said. "I admire your moxie. I'll take what you got here. Here are your pads."

Caroline forced herself to look him in the face. "Thank you, sir."

"I want you to promise me one thing, though."

"Sir?"

"I want you to show them boys up, y'hear?"

She smiled and straightened her shoulders. "I'll do my best."

As she left, she heard Mr. Reider telling someone—perhaps a stock boy in the back— about the crazy girl who wanted to play hockey.

A curious sensation spread through her. This was *excitement*. This was *exhilaration*. And she realized that she hadn't felt anything like it in a long, long while. Probably not since she'd kissed Joseph right out on the sidewalk.

It was a lovely feeling, and Caroline relished everything about it. And she liked everything about her hockey gear, too. She liked the way the long sock stretched from her toe, unrolling as it went, over her shin, all the way up to her knee. She even liked the smell of it; the years of sweat and dirt and use and wear a potpourri of staleness. And yet it smelled good, the scent of excitement. She was nervous. She hadn't been practicing. But she hoped that instinct would take over the moment she hit the ice.

After she dressed, she presented herself to her mother, who managed a smile. It was an unreadable smile, though, one Caroline hadn't seen from her mother before. Some odd mixture of grief, pride, love, distance, all wrapped up in one.

"How do I look?" Caroline asked.

"You certainly look …" Mrs. Panski trailed off, mid-thought, and then didn't recover that thought, as if it had floated away.

After a moment more, Caroline no longer waited. She knew how difficult is was for her mother, so she didn't push it. "You're not coming with me to tryouts, are you?"

"I've got Sam," was the response.

There was no reason Sam couldn't accompany them, and they both knew it. Given the choice, Sam would undoubtedly have liked to go along. He loved riding the trolley and would take any excuse to do so. But there'd been a strange distance since her mother had given her the tryout notice.

Caroline's mom had been more than quiet, and she'd often kept her gaze averted. Every time Caroline mentioned hockey, Mrs. Panski steered the conversation elsewhere, as if she hadn't heard her daughter correctly. When Caroline said, "I can't wait to get out on the ice, show those boys what I can do," her mother replied, "Honey, can you hand me that dish towel, please? And don't forget to put away the folded laundry I put next to your bureau."

So Caroline resigned herself to going alone. And why not? At first, she was hurt—after all, her mother was the one who had suggested it in the first place. But Caroline knew this was her adventure in any case. Hers and hers alone. To win or lose, but at least to try.

Once she had on all of her pads, she kissed her mom goodbye and headed out, her hands in oversize gloves, the stick heaved over her shoulder like a hobo's kit bag. Her skates rested over her other shoulder. She'd put them on when she got to tryouts. But she looked forward to that, too, the roiling gait, the short mincing steps as she headed out onto the ice.

At the trolley stop, she was a spectacle. She may as well have been a blue whale out for a stroll. This young girl, puffed up in her pads, her long hair tied up in a sloppy bun with its loose strands dipping over her neck and shoulders. It was an incongruous sight for sure, and those waiting for the trolley didn't even bother to hide their curiosity. They gawked, unembarrassed. Little kids, tethered to their mothers by gloved, clutching hands, some of them with snot trails adorning their upper lips, just stared as if Jesus himself had arisen from the dead and stood waiting to hitch a ride on the Number 9 to North Avenue.

Some people smiled at her, but none of these smiles were of encouragement or for an appreciation of her chutzpah. They were, instead, discerning, judgmental, patronizing smiles. Smiles that said, "Are you serious?"

Caroline expected this from the men, with their folded newspapers and cigarettes and their cheap hats and blazers. But from the women, too? Shouldn't there have existed some feminine bond that oozed encouragement? One lady, right across the row from her on the trolley, actually scowled. She was a young woman, no older than Caroline's own mother, and they locked eyes for a moment before Caroline, as was her place and station as the younger, had to look away.

The disapproving looks threatened to overpower her excitement altogether. And Caroline needed that excitement, needed the adrenaline to pump her up. Because when it left, a nagging sense of doubt remained in its wake. And that was the last thing she needed. If she was honest with herself, she harbored enough doubt just below the surface to last her a lifetime.

As the trolley approached the shadow of the hulking Sports Center building, it was almost too much to bear. She realized now that she'd failed to fully consider the reality of what was ahead, despite the blatant stares of her cowardly fellow citizens. Sure, she knew intellectually that she'd be the only girl. But what that meant, and what was in store for her because of that fact—that was something she had simply failed to absorb or examine. Now was the moment of truth.

She realized that it was primarily the sense of duty she felt she had to her father that kept her going, that prevented her from pulling the trolley cord way too early, skipping the stop, and heading right back home. Trying out for a boys' hockey team was actually a terrifying prospect.

It would be so much easier to do what other girls her age were doing. She should be dismantling any thoughts of rebellion or lack of convention and simply slot herself into the well-worn grooves of expectation. She should finish school, find a man, get engaged, get married, have children, keep a home, and take her place in the carousel of the American Dream. Why should it be different for her? Why did she do the things she did? She had no answers to those questions—no answers apart from some vague notion that pursuing crazy dreams was something her father would want for her.

"You can do anything you want to do," she recalled him telling her, and when she looked at that stick and saw the Clippers logo there, well, it felt as if her father was sitting there next to her on the trolley. And that was enough to sustain her as she headed into the building and presented herself at the tryouts.

The reaction was predictable enough. Everyone stopped and stared at her. At *her*. She was a *she*. Here, at a tryout for a hockey team. Some of the boys gawked. Others laughed outright. When the coach spotted her putting on her skates, he removed the whistle from his mouth and scrutinized her, saving his longest appraisal for her hair.

"This for real?" he asked.

Somewhere, from deep inside, in a voice she hardly recognized as her own, she managed, "Yes, sir. This is for real."

By way of response, the coach flashed an amused grin and then blew the whistle. "Everyone on the ice," he shouted.

All the kids, two dozen of them, spilled onto the rink. It was like a funnel and they bumped into one another. Caroline took a hit and tipped on the edge of her skates, threatening to topple before righting herself with a flail of her arms.

"Sorry," came a deep voice, and then a boy's outstretched arm reached for her, steadying her.

With his help, she regained her balance. "It's okay," she said, but really she felt like she was going to throw up. Nerves. "I'm okay," she repeated, more for her own convincing than for his.

And then she looked up and recognized his face. At least she thought she recognized it. She stared at him. Yes, there was something in the face, in the eyes. She definitely recognized him. But from where?

"Caroline Panski," the guy said through a big smile. "I should have known."

She just looked at him.

"Alan Petrauskas," he said.

Alan Petrauskas! The creep who hit her on the pond. The idiot she walloped the day she found out her dad died. The jerk who beat up Joseph and then disappeared afterward. The absolute living scum. A feeling of disgust rose up in Caroline's chest. Bad enough she had to prove herself to a bunch of idiot boys, but to think Alan Petrauskas would be one of them. Ugh.

"Let's go, boys," the coach bellowed. "Line up. Far side. Skates and sticks up!"

Getting reacquainted, as distasteful as it would be, would have to wait.

The first exercises were easy enough—one line feeding pucks to the other, one-timer shots after receiving the pass, then switch lines. Caroline did well enough. Cross rink passes were a piece of cake, and one-timer shots were no problem, either. She failed to get solid contact on most of them, but she never whiffed, as several others did. Alan, she noticed, was terrific. He wound up and got solid wood on every slapshot, sending each hurtling into the netting. His only miss clanged against the post.

Next came sprints from blue line to blue line, back and forth, with no indication of when they might rest. Chest heaving, sweat soaking her hair, Caroline could feel the burn in her legs, the throbbing of her feet in her skates. She couldn't help but notice Alan excelled here, too. He was the first one to the far line, first one back, again and again until he'd actually lapped several of the other players. Little wonder; he must have been pushing six feet tall with broad shoulders and a jaw both squared and dimpled. Sweating copiously, his hair had fallen in dark cords across his forehead. He was breathing heavily when coach finally called for a water break. One of the boys dry heaved into a trash can, but within moments, Alan looked ready to take to the ice again.

But the coach hadn't called them out yet and as the players chugged their water and tried to recuperate, one of the boys, a mealy-mouthed kid with a constellation of pimples across his cheeks, pointed to Caroline's stick and laughed.

"Look at that thing. Ain't even a real stick."

Practice had been so intense to that point

that none of the other boys had any real opportunity to home in on this easy mark. But now,
it proved irresistible. "That thing is flimsy," one
of them said. "Let me see that," said another as
he yanked it out of Caroline's hands.

A fiery shiver shot up her spine. She had
long ago, in some deep intractable way, mentally morphed her very own father onto the
face of the Clippers captain on her stick.
They looked nothing alike, of course, the old
grizzled sea captain and her handsome young
father. But, still, to see him manhandled this
way, mocked and ridiculed, it was too much.
She blinked away the blind fury clouding her
vision and made a move for her stick. But she
was too late. Alan already had the stick in his
hands.

"That isn't yours," he said to the twerp
who took it away. "Besides, it's pretty cool," he
added, handing it back to Caroline.

No one dared challenge Alan, who had
already established himself as the leader of the
team. Caroline didn't know what to do or say.

She had once loathed Alan, but he'd clearly gone through a transformation. Was that what military school did to you? He was, apparently, polite—and gorgeous. What on earth had happened to him?

Still, Caroline hadn't forgotten how much of a jerk he'd been in the past, so she took her stick back without saying thanks. There was little time for expressions of gratitude in any case. The coach ordered everyone back onto the ice for more drills. It went on this way for another hour before the coach called it quits and told everyone to come back tomorrow if they hadn't had enough.

Caroline took her time leaving the ice. She sat down and leaned against a wall, watching the boys slowly make their way off the ice. They were too gassed to say anything else, each boy apparently too tired to worry too much about a girl. Besides, while she was far from the best, she clearly wasn't the worst, either.

"Coming back tomorrow?" Alan asked as he skated past.

Caroline nodded, but didn't look up. Unconsciously, she rubbed her fingers back and forth over her stick's Clippers logo.

When she got home, Caroline dropped her equipment next to the door and slumped into the big red chair. Mrs. Panski leaned out of the kitchen, and said, "Get washed up. Supper's ready," and then disappeared back into the kitchen.

Caroline dragged herself out of the chair to the dinner table. She didn't say a word during the meal. She even nodded off once.

"What's the matter?" Mrs. Panski asked.

"I'm exhausted."

"Well then, finish up and get on to bed."

Caroline took her dishes into the kitchen, pushed in her chair, and dragged herself upstairs. She barely made it through brushing her teeth and hair before she collapsed into bed, too exhausted even to crawl under the sheets and blankets. She was grateful for the exhaustion. It allowed her mind to go blank, which was a very good thing. When everything was reduced to the physical, it meant that nothing else got through. The physical—muscles, tendons, bones—she could rely on. It was all the other stuff that got in the way and made life messy.

Later, Mrs. Panski tugged on the sheets and blankets, untangled them, and pulled them up over her still-sleeping daughter. Then she bent and kissed Caroline on the head and turned out the light.

22

WHERE THERE HAD BEEN two dozen or more kids at tryouts the day before, on the second day there were fewer than twenty. From the moment she got out of bed, Caroline had felt the soreness from her toes to her shoulders, but some twelve hours of sleep had healed the minor aches and pains, and after moving around a bit, she'd worked out the worst of the kinks. Besides, the soreness felt good. It felt like she was doing something real again.

But once she was out on the ice, replaying the drills from the day before, executing the same moves, putting the same pressures on the same points—quick twists and turns and "ankle-breaker" drills—she could feel every inch of herself, and every inch hurt.

She even considered quitting once, when a tight twitch in her left calf embedded itself in her muscle and burrowed deep, almost into the bone. It was a subterranean hurt, a bottomless bruise that she knew would not work itself out anytime soon.

It would be easy to quit. She could blame it on the muscle bruise. It would be easy to convince herself that she'd given it her best shot, that she didn't see it through because, after all, her calf betrayed her. She could tell herself, in all honesty, that it wasn't due to lack of effort.

But quitting was more difficult than carrying on. She wished it wasn't that way, but it was. She'd shut down most of the previous year, and now that her switch had been turned back on, she wasn't ready to turn it back off.

"You all right?"

Caroline looked up from kneading her calf to see Alan standing over her.

"Yeah. I'm all right," she said and promptly stood and hopped back on the ice. She skated over to take her turn in line for a drill where two players raced into the corner to dig out a puck. She wasn't sure why she'd said she was okay. She wasn't. It hurt. Bad. But she didn't want to tell Alan that. She didn't want him to know.

It had been over a year since they'd been out on the pond together, and yet, in some palpable way, she was still fighting out there. But fighting something different now, something she didn't quite understand. Back then, it was all so obvious. Alan was a creep and he deserved to lose his teeth. But now? She found that she wanted to impress him, show him what she was made of. But this time, it was for very different reasons.

During the first break, the two of them sat on the far end of the bench, the other players congregated nearer the midlines.

"Is it a cramp?" he asked, after observing her limp off the ice.

She shrugged. "I guess so."

They were both silent awhile, still breathing heavily from the exertion.

"So, where did you disappear to?" she asked finally, deciding that it was too much effort to stay mad at him. Clearly, he was a different person now, and he was trying to be nice.

"You mean after you knocked out my tooth?" He smiled as he said this, which allowed her to smile at the recollection, too. Besides, she could see he had a mouth full of teeth, in two perfect rows. The little nugget that had loosed itself from his gum and skittered across the ice must have been one of the last of his babies. "I went to Nottingham Academy, up in Aberdeen."

She'd heard he'd gone to military school and guessed that Nottingham must be the name. "Why would you do that?" she asked.

"Not much choice in the matter."

"Oh."

"I was pretty mad at my dad at first. All the way up there. Took two hours on the bus. I couldn't believe we were still in Maryland. But it was good for me."

"You got to keep playing hockey, obviously."

"We have a great rink up there. I was captain of the team last year."

"You're really good."

"You're not so bad yourself."

Caroline smiled.

But it was short-lived. Soon they were back out on the ice, and that familiar old burn followed.

That night there was no time to think about Alan and his transformation. Her aching toes were barely under the sheets and her head barely on the pillow before Caroline passed out cold. This was the pattern each night of the week, and the time progressed with Caroline moving through it increasingly zombie-like.

Each day she woke, pulled herself through breakfast, hauled her gear along the trolley line—she was no longer conscious of the stares, choosing to ignore them and too tired to care anyway—arrived at the Sports Center, ignored Coach's malevolent smile, and then hit the ice in yet another seemingly impossible turn. It was the sort of numb otherness she imagined her father might have faced in combat, a strange combination of switching off your brain and moving through the world on autopilot, relying on reaction and instinct even as your senses were sharply attuned, hyper-aware even.

She swore that on the trolley ride she could hear the crackle of the electric wires, smell the peppermint chewing gum from other riders, feel every solitary little bump and ruffle on the line, continuing even after she got off, feeling each pebble on the sidewalk. It was the same thing out on the ice. A whoosh of air from a passing player felt like a burst. Whispered grunts turned into shouts. Slight brushes of an opponent's jersey felt as if someone had thrown a soaked woolen sweater at her, landing with a hard thud against her aching body.

And then it was over, just at the very moment, it seemed, that her body was ready to give up and her toes threatened to explode from pain. Then, she did the trolley trip in reverse, staggered up the stoop to her house, dropped her gear by the front door, and slumped into the red chair. Each night, her mother poked her head out of the kitchen and registered Caroline's presence—"Oh, you're home. Well, get washed up"—and Caroline dutifully did, a machine fit now only to take orders.

She managed her way through dinners, head on her hand, ignoring Sam, ignoring the world, ignoring her taste buds even, mechanically shoveling in the food, for she was ravenously hungry, but failing to register any of it, before falling into bed to do it all again the following day.

And then, amazingly, somehow, the final day of tryouts arrived. She'd lasted the entire week. In fact, she realized as she ate breakfast that morning, she actually felt better physically than she had since day one. She'd done her best and would have no regrets. And yet this wasn't some silly lark. This wasn't a situation in which she could pat herself on the back for a job well done, knowing she hadn't made the team but proved some point anyway, a shout to the world that a girl could do whatever a boy could. No, she deserved a slot on the team.

And when she arrived on the last day Caroline saw that only sixteen of the boys remained. And there would be at least fifteen roster slots, if not sixteen, meaning maybe everybody would make it. After practice, Coach announced that the posted list with final cuts would be hanging outside his office door. "Get cleaned up," he said, "And then check your assignment."

Caroline was confident as they made their way to Coach's office. She even joined the boys in lighthearted banter and joshing, ribbing one of the guys for his whiff when they practiced penalty shots. And, it seemed, the boys had accepted her. They appeared to have forgotten she was a girl, or they finally didn't care. Suddenly, the prospect of making the team, of having survived the weeklong ordeal, had equalized them all. Such pettiness as gender wasn't part of the deal. Plus, in looking at the numbers, they all knew they'd be offered a roster spot anyway, secure in the knowledge that for three nights a week for the next few months, they would be back here, practicing with the squad. They'd be hockey players.

At first, she couldn't decipher the looks on the boys' faces as they scanned the list. Then she recognized it. It was a look of consideration. It looked, in some weird way, not all that different from the awful expressions the army men wore when they came to tell her about her father.

At first, there surfaced a strange ripple of protection. They literally shielded her from seeing the list before some unspoken current between them made them step aside, allowing her to move through them almost like some grim receiving line. And then they were all standing behind her, watching as it dawned on the girl—she was a girl again now; no one could forget that, not ever—that hers was the only name not on the list.

The boys seemed to dissolve, fizzle away. It was just her now, standing alone in the hall outside the coach's office.

She bit back the tears, aware that crying would only provide Coach with confirmation of his decision. Then she pulled herself together, and, hesitating just a moment, banged her fist on the door.

The door flung open, and there he stood, whistle still dangling around his neck. He stared at her, and Caroline stared back, a silent showdown.

"Can I help you, Panski?"

There in the bowels of the Sports Center, a hideous cinder block office like a jail cell, Caroline Panski, not yet thirteen years old, demanded an explanation.

He told her to come in, have a seat. The office smelled terrible, due to the disgusting, sodden-end cigar he had clutched between his teeth. He didn't even bother to remove the revolting thing from his mouth as he talked.

"I only have fifteen slots," he explained.

"Someone had to get cut. Besides, Jones might be joining us after all."

Jones. Dennis Jones. A good player, but someone who'd disappeared after the third day.

"And that would make sixteen."

"That's right."

"So why not sixteen now?"

"Because then Jones would make seventeen. Too many." He chuckled as he said this, as if he was incredulous that this kid couldn't perform rudimentary mathematics.

"This isn't fair," Caroline blurted, even though she didn't want to. She wanted to remain in control, send hammer blows against this stupid guy's illogic.

"The world ain't fair, sweetheart. Hey, you made a good effort. You should be proud."

"I deserve to be on the team. Third line, fine. But I deserve it."

"I admire your spunk, so I'm gonna be straight with you." He took a deep draw on the cigar, letting the smoke linger in his airway before pushing out a slow, languid stream of nastiness. "This is a boys' team. You're a girl. See the problem here?"

"Then why let me come every day? Why have me go through all that?"

"I figured you wouldn't make it past the first day. I said that every day until the week ended."

"But I did make it past the first day. And the second. And the third, and—"

"As I said, I admire your spunk."

There was little point continuing such a ridiculous conversation. She looked at his desk, the sparse tableau of an ugly man. A chipped coffee mug, dried brown spots clinging to the rim and handle. A pile of mimeographed papers, curled at the edges. A magazine with a scantily dressed woman on the cover. She hardly knew what she was doing and would have been shocked by it if she wasn't so angry, but as she started to walk out, she turned back toward the coach and slid her arm across his desk, sending his things flying and spilling coffee across his desk and shirt.

"Hey!" he yelled, scrambling backward.

But she was already out the door.

One's station in life—had the message not been clear before—was a cruel thing dictated not by will, but by circumstance, accidents of time and place.

Soon, she was outside, the sun that had shone so brightly that morning now blotted out by thick, menacing clouds. During times like these, as she had so many times before, she thought of Joseph.

23

CAROLINE WAS THE PICTURE of nervous energy, vacillating between keeping her eyes down in front of her and stealthily looking up, searching for something, checking out houses as she passed. The houses were narrower, more rundown than in her neighborhood. Every sixth or seventh house was boarded up. She couldn't recall it being this bad the last time she came.

This was certainly not her neighborhood; that much was clear. It was not where she belonged. One look at her and nothing could be more obvious. But her skin color gave her access that others, like Joseph, didn't get to share. She turned a corner and crossed East Eager, then another block. She wasn't even sure if she'd come to the right place. But maybe it was just that the world was different, and all its sceneries and all its sets had changed along with it.

It had gone poorly when she'd come last time, so why come back?

Well, why not? What was there to lose? She told herself that there had been two things important to her over the last couple of years. Two things—besides her family—that had defined her: hockey and Joseph. She'd tried the first one. Tried and, well, not quite failed. But hadn't succeeded, either. So now it was time for the other.

She reached Wolfe Street and paused for a bit before the house, or what she thought was the house: #1104. But the houses all looked the same to her. The same bricks piled one atop the other, the same filthy stoops, the same windows in the same spots, the same gauzy curtains behind them. But then she spotted the plaster tree branch above the door and remembered. It was just that it looked so much more solid, cleaner, more welcoming the last time. Now the door and windows seemed to make up a crooked leering face, ready to swallow her whole if she came any closer.

But she inhaled deeply, climbed the stoop, and stepped to the door and knocked. No vicious barking this time. No calls from inside. Nothing. She debated whether to walk away or knock again. She stood there, was about to turn, when the door opened.

"Yes?"

There stood an elderly black woman, her hair set in brightly colored plastic curlers. She wore a blue robe, cinched up to her neck. The old woman put a pair of large black glasses to her face. If Caroline was reading this right, the woman looked even more nervous and unsure than Caroline imagined she herself looked.

"Help you?" the woman asked, still shielding half her body behind the door.

"Yes. I was wondering. I'm sorry to bother you. I was wondering . . ."

"Yes?"

"I'm looking for Joseph Wilson. Does he live here?"

"No, miss, he does not."

"Do you know where he moved?"

"No, miss, I do not. What I do know is that I've been in this house with my George for seven months now."

"Yes, ma'am."

"Who's that?" came a bellowing voice from inside the house.

"White girl. Looking for old tenants."

The door opened up more and there appeared a lumbering, gargantuan man—gray hair and ponderous belly. "What you want, little girl?"

"I told you already," said the lady. "She's looking for the old tenants. Wilsons, I think she said."

"Yes, ma'am. Joseph Wilson."

"Well, they don't live here no more," the man said.

"And that is exactly what I told her already."

The couple engaged in what appeared to be a well-worn drizzle of little nags, only stopping when they noticed Caroline had walked down the stoop and was making her way along the sidewalk, a small figure receding into the distance.

"Where have you been?" Mrs. Panski asked when Caroline got home, at least an hour after she had been expected and well after the sun had set.

"Oh, Mama," she said. But that was as far she got. Her determination to hold it all in was no match for the flood of release. Out it came, in torrents, long gusts of sobbing, punctuated by quick bursts of tears and coughs. She didn't tell her mother anything about Joseph, of course—there was nothing to be gained in that. She told her instead of the other great failure, the rejection down at the hockey rink. She would not be offered a spot on the team, even though there were going to be no more cuts, and even though she had made it through the entire week. It just wasn't fair.

"No, the world is not fair, sweetheart," Mrs. Panski concurred. "But you can take comfort in knowing that you did your best. No one can ever take that away from you."

"What do you mean? They did take it away from me. And I'll never get it back."

Mrs. Panski had no response. Her child was right, after all, and she knew that all too well.

24

"MY STOMACH HURTS," Caroline said.

Mrs. Panski placed her hand on Caroline's forehead. "You don't feel warm . . . is it that you just want to stay home from school?"

Caroline didn't answer.

Mrs. Panski got up. "Just this one time."

Caroline noticed that her mother was dressed more formally than usual—she had donned a blue skirt and sweater, even put on a string of small pearls—and certainly more so than if she was just going to be sitting in the house. And what else did her mother do during the day, really? Caroline never knew.

"Where are you going?" Caroline asked.

Mrs. Panski hesitated. "Nowhere. I have a few errands to run. I'm going to the grocer's."

"Can I come?"

"I thought you were sick."

Caroline didn't say anything.

"If you're too sick to go to school, then you are to do nothing but lay here. You can read if you want. I won't be too long. For now, I suggest you go back to sleep, little sickie."

"OK."

But the moment her mother left the house, Caroline leapt out of bed and peered out the window, watching as Mrs. Panski made her way down the sidewalk—in the opposite direction from the grocer's. Caroline spent half a second wondering why before she jumped into her clothes and followed her mother out the door. Quickly, she caught up to within a hundred feet or so, far enough away to remain undetected but close enough to watch her mother halt at the trolley stop.

As Mrs. Panski got on the front, Caroline sprinted to the back door and slipped in between two grown men. She stood in the well and then slowly peered over to see her mother taking a seat at the front. Caroline found an empty space in the back and quickly grabbed a newspaper left behind by another rider. She slipped the paper in front of her face, pretending to read, garnering smiles from the adult riders near her, and occasionally looked over the paper at her mother who sat, unmoving, through some ten stops before she got up and exited. Caroline stayed on, afraid of being spotted, but she knew the stop right away. The Sports Center was just down the block.

Caroline got off at the next stop and doubled her way back toward the Sports Center. Sprinting there, she reached the building quickly enough, but found no one outside. She slipped in the front door and walked slowly down the hall, toward the ice. She could hear the sounds of men out on the rink practicing.

She ducked behind two large trash cans when she spotted her mother, standing near the ice. Just standing there. Standing and watching. What on earth was she doing? Was she envisioning that clumsy woman who'd injured her, years earlier, on this very ice? The "oaf" as Mrs. Panski had called her when she related the story to Caroline? The popping sound? The weird, irregular way her leg moved in the immediate years after the injury, as if pieces of her were shifting one on top of another, deep inside, leaving her with the limp that was now her most prominent feature?

Caroline watched as a man approached Mrs. Panski and asked, in a gruff tone, if he could help her.

"Where's the youth coach?" Mrs. Panski demanded. From the sound of her tone, she was apparently content to meet this guy's rudeness with her own.

"Is there something I can help you with?"

"I need to speak with the youth coach."

"About what, may I ask?"

"Are you the coach?"

"No. He's in his office. Is he expecting you?"

"No."

"He might be busy."

"If he is, I can wait."

The guy huffed out an exasperated breath, but said, "Follow me," and the two of them walked down the hall with Caroline not far behind. "In here," the guy said when they reached the coach's door. Caroline ducked into the ladies bathroom, listening to the squeak of the guy's shoes on the linoleum floor, getting quieter and quieter as he got further and further away. Satisfied that he'd gone, Caroline tiptoed to just outside the coach's door, where he heard his voice.

"Yes, ma'am. How can I help you?"

And then her mother: "I'm Eloise Panski"

Then Coach again: "I've got a lot of work to do."

Caroline knew what that office looked like, and she knew her mother would be hating it there, that she'd probably seen the magazine and everything.

"Caroline Panski is my daughter."

"Yes. Fine player."

"For a girl?'

"Yes, that's right. For a girl."

"I believe she's a fine player for a boy, too."

"Perhaps that's true."

"If that's true, then why isn't she on your team?"

Caroline repositioned herself. Now she was able to see inside, the back of her mother and the coach behind her, his face obscured by Mrs. Panski's hair. She watched as the coach reached for a drawer in his desk. Sliding it open, he retrieved a nasty cigar and began some laborious attempts at lighting it. It was no easy business, eating up three matches and a full minute before he was successful. The foul odor was instantaneous. Almost immediately, an acrid gray smoke swirled around the closed-in room. Mrs. Panski coughed, twice, stifling both in her clenched hand.

"Did you see the players out there on the ice when you came in?"

"I did."

"And did you discern what they all have in common?"

"I did."

"Well, there were no females out there," Coach said, stating the obvious.

"And did you know that there used to be a women's league? Played their games on that very ice?" Eloise asked.

The coach reached into the drawer again, this time pulling out an old yellowed paper. "In fact, I did know that. Here, look at this," he said. "Spitfires, 1937." He tossed the program across the desk. Mrs. Panski took a look at it.

Caroline smiled. She knew her mother would be in that program, and she knew the coach had no idea.

"That's me," Mrs. Panski said, pointing to the woman in the back row, muffled in her goalie gear. Caroline could see the program, held aloft in her mother's hand, before the coach snapped it back, stared at it, at her, at the picture, at the woman in front of him.

"Well, I'll be," he finally muttered.

"Let me ask you, is she a decent player? And I don't mean, 'for a girl.' I mean is she a decent player?"

"She is. One of the weaker, to be sure. But she can play."

"Then she deserves a spot on your team."

"This isn't like that," he said, pointing to the program. "We compete. We play against other teams. There's a championship involved. And my teams have won them four of the last six years."

"And her being on the team will prevent that? Is that what you're saying?"

"What I'm saying is that she's a girl. And she'll be playing against boys. And she'll most likely get hurt."

Mrs. Panski was quiet. From where Caroline stood, it looked as if maybe her mother had winced at this. Of course, there was some truth to it, and it must have hurt her mother to hear it. But she knew her mother had already thought about the possibility of Caroline getting hurt just like the coach said. Just like she used to say, only weeks earlier.

She wanted to burst through the door, assure her mother—and the coach—that she wouldn't get hurt. And that anyway, it was worth the risk. But she stayed where she was, waiting, listening, wondering what her mother would say.

At first Mrs. Panski said nothing. Just sat there in silence. She stifled another cough, the cigar emitting a steady stream of heavy gray smoke that never seemed to rise, but rather hovered, lending a gauzy film to the room.

Caroline thought maybe her mother would just get up and leave, defeated, just like Caroline herself had been. But just as quickly, she knew otherwise. She knew why her mother was there, why she'd come in the first place. She was there because Caroline deserved the chance. Because Caroline lost her father. Because Caroline wanted to be friends with Joseph, and she couldn't do that, either. Because, in the end, her mother believed that Caroline should have more opportunities than she had herself.

"Let me ask you something," Mrs. Panski finally said. "Do you believe, do you believe for one split second, that you are more concerned about Caroline getting hurt than I am, her own mother?"

"Of course not, no."

"Okay, then. I'm glad you agree that you are not more concerned about my daughter's welfare than I am. Now, that being the case, if that concern was the only reason for you not putting her on this team, then you have my blessing to reconsider that decision and go ahead and offer her a roster spot."

Coach drew in a breath and shook his head. He smiled. "Okay, okay," he said, his hands raised in mock surrender, the movement scattering a particularly languid cloud of smoke. "You win. She's on the team."

Caroline didn't know how to feel about this. She appreciated what her mother was doing for her. But on the other hand, she wanted to earn the spot herself, and she wanted to do it without any help. That was the whole point.

Eloise gathered her purse and rose from the uncomfortable chair.

Caroline stepped back and took off down the hall. As she passed the ice, she saw one of the larger men smashing a guy against the boards. The assistant coach blew a whistle and everyone stopped, watching as the guy tried to collect himself off the ground. Eventually, the coach and one of the other players helped him off the ice, moving slowly as the guy favored his left leg and hung his head. He had a dazed look in his eyes as he took his place on the bench. Caroline kept going, bursting out of the Sports Center and into the sunlight.

25

THE FIRST PRACTICE with the boys arrived, and Caroline didn't want to be nervous. She wanted to believe that she had no reason to be nervous, that she belonged here, that she'd earned it. But she knew that on some fundamental level that wasn't true. She was on the team because her mother had paid a visit to the coach. When Mrs. Panski first came home to tell Caroline the news, Caroline was back in her bed and under the covers.

She'd pasted a confused look on her face. "What do you mean I'm on the team?"

"You're on the team." Mrs. Panski delivered this announcement with a smile on her face, but it was what Caroline and Sam called their mother's "sad smile." The lips were upturned, yes, but that was it. No movement of the eyebrows or the lines around her mouth. No spark in the eyes. It was a smile they'd seen a lot of in recent years.

"But how?" Caroline asked.

"I spoke with the coach."

"And what did you say?"

"That's not important. What's important is that he's agreed to put you on the team."

"But I didn't want to make the team that way. I wanted to make it because I earned it."

"I think you did earn it. I think you were good enough to be on the team. The coach suggested as much. And he said that if you were a boy you would have been on it. So, to me, that seems you did earn it."

"But it's only because you went and spoke with him. I wish you hadn't done that."

"I'm sorry. If you don't want to show up for practice, I'll respect that."

Caroline followed her mother downstairs where Mrs. Panski grabbed a magazine and sat down. She stared intently at it, turning the pages so rapidly that Caroline knew there was no way she was actually reading it. She wanted to say something to her mother, or have her mother say something more to her, but things felt very final. The decision was Caroline's: go to practice or don't go to practice. It was simple. And yet it was not simple at all.

Conflicting emotions swirled within her, feelings that didn't have a name. It was true that she didn't want her mother's help. She'd wanted to earn a spot on her own. And yet, she had to acknowledge the bigger truth that she was, after all, a girl, and the world was a place that didn't bend itself so easily to the wills of girls. Sometimes, girls needed help.

She didn't know what to say or do, so she went back to her room. There, she saw her skates and stick, the wooden handle tucked inside the right skate, the curved end leaning against the wall. Even if she accepted the help given her, it would still be up to her to get out there and earn it on the ice, show the coach and all the other boys that she was there because she was good. That was the reason she was on the team. She'd show 'em.

She went back downstairs.

"Mama?"

Mrs. Panski was still in the same chair, but she was staring straight ahead, into space, the magazine closed and on her lap.

"Yes?"

"I'll play."

"Okay."

"And, Mama?"

"Yes?"

"Thank you."

Mrs. Panski smiled, and this time, it came close to her real smile. Not entirely there, but close. Very close.

When she walked in the door at the Sports Center, Caroline was immediately struck by the smell. It was a familiar, sickly potpourri of sweat, stale beer, and old building. Caroline imagined that it smelled exactly like it had back in the days when her mother played on this same rink. She thought of how her mother had described the old galleys where the benches were so close to the audience that people used to spill beer on the players. That hadn't changed. She imagined how difficult it must have been for her mom to step inside this place, to speak with Coach, and see the boys out on the ice.

Certainly she'd been by the Sports Center a few times over the years. Hard to remain in Baltimore and not at least pass by it once or twice—on the bus, perhaps, or on some errand that took her to a part of the city she didn't usually frequent. So, yes, she'd seen it. But she hadn't been inside. Not since the injury. Caroline was sure of that.

And so coming back must have been ex-cruciating, to have had to smell that smell again. Because it smelled like competition and freedom and youth. Caroline knew that her mother had played her heart out in those years, and had enjoyed it immensely. And all that was gone now. And so Caroline decided she was playing, in part, for her mom.

And for her dad.

And of course, for herself.

"Look who's here!" Alan. It was amazing what time had done to him, Caroline thought for probably the hundredth time. In essence, he'd uttered that same phrase—Look who's here!—to her back at the pond, but back then it was mocking, full of venom and spite. Now he had a smile on his face and he looked welcoming.

"Hi," Caroline said.

He looked down at her. Even without skates, he was tall. He used to be a shrimp. She used to tower over him. But even then he was broad. And he was broader still now. Some of the other boys passed by them, but no one said anything to Caroline.

"I heard you're on the team cause your mom came and yelled at Coach," Alan said.

"That's not exactly true."

"I didn't think so. I told the guys you're on the team cause you're better'n most of them."

She looked down. "I'm not sure that's true, either."

But then a shrill whistle blew and the pleasantries were over. It was Coach. "Let's go, boys," he announced. "Practice starts in ten minutes."

They headed to the locker rooms: fifteen boys in one direction, one girl in the other. It was eerily quiet in the locker room alone. Even though she knew no one was there with her, Caroline kept looking around nervously. It felt like anyone could walk in at any moment. But no one did, and she needed to hurry. So she got dressed, trying hard not to think about how things would go on the ice. She tried to visualize success.

"I've got to trust myself," she whispered. She felt a little silly talking to herself, but there was no one else there and she needed a pep talk. "Let instincts take over. If I'm concentrating on not messing up, I'm going to forget how to play. I can't think too much about technique. I just have to let myself move on the ice. I just have to play the game." She got up and headed out.

Once she hit the ice, there was no time to think anyway. Just like at tryouts, the coach demanded attention and precision, and practice proved just as hard as tryouts had been. By the first water break, Caroline was drenched in sweat. She poured half her water down the back of her neck and felt the relief it brought when it slithered all the way down to her T-shirt and underwear and to the tips of her toes.

Alan mashed his hand on her back. "I do that, too," he said. "With the water. Feels good, doesn't it?"

Caroline nodded. Again, the mysteries of this world. It hadn't been that long ago when the prospect of Alan touching her, even through the thickness of shirt and sweater, would have repulsed her. But now the pressure of his hand felt good, like some kind of strange security in a place where she still felt on edge, still felt as if any moment the whistle would blow and the boys would refuse to play with her, realizing that, geez, that kid with the corny replica stick is a girl.

Nerves did get to her, regardless. She didn't perform near her best and Coach got on her. "Come on, Panski," he yelled several times. And when she did mess up, Alan didn't bother to try and make her feel better. He was, after all, concentrating on his own play and as the team's best player and its captain, he had to set an example. It was as if his job of making Caroline feel welcome was complete. The rest was up to her.

But she couldn't get it together enough to impress the coach or her teammates, and so she didn't get any playing time when the games started. During the team's first game, against Mount Saint Joseph's, she sat on the bench, at times losing herself in the action, calling out encouragement to her teammates, and waiting for her name to get called.

And then the game was over, an 8-1 slaughter. The coach fumed. She could hear him all the way down the hall as he chewed out the boys for their sloppy, lethargic play. She could still hear the rise of his voice even as she entered her own locker room. But she didn't need to shower. She just got back into her clothes and left.

And nothing changed the next time, either—nothing but the score, a loss again, but a more respectable 6-3. Again, she sat on the bench and again her name wasn't called. She'd stopped cheering her teammates by the middle of the second period. When the game was over, and the players trudged off the ice and toward the locker room, Caroline realized her stick was gone. She panicked.

"Anyone seen my stick?" she asked. No one answered. She asked Coach, and his response was only a growling, "How the hell would I know?" as he marched into the locker room.

She stood in the hallway and listened again as Coach yelled at the boys. When he finished and everyone spilled out into the hall, she marched up to Coach and demanded that her teammates give her the stick back. "My father gave me that stick," she said, tears welling in her eyes, standing there before the boys in their street clothes. They just looked at her, saying nothing. Even Alan was quiet.

"You should all be ashamed of yourselves," she yelled and turned away so they wouldn't see her cry.

Outside, a gray mist hung in the air, turning the entire sky into a gauzy mess. It matched Caroline's mood. She looked at the bleak scene around her. There was no one out and about. It looked like someone had come along and tipped the world over and all the people had simply fallen away. She had thoughts of the entire building collapsing behind her, coming down on those jerks inside. She was as good as most of them. She knew that. And just because she was born one way and they were born another, they got to do whatever they wanted and she got to do nothing she wanted.

It wasn't fair. Wouldn't it have been better to have accepted the decision in the first place, blame it on an unfair society that disallowed girls the same opportunities it held for boys? Wouldn't it have been better to quit while behind instead of having to endure a further, and double, humiliation? And now her beloved stick was gone. It was almost too much to bear. She had lost her dad once already and now, well, she just couldn't think about it. It was all too much.

Why fight the universe? It was so very, very tiring. All that was left to do now was go home.

26

CAROLINE DIDN'T GO to practice the next day. Or the day after that. She told her mother she didn't feel good and her mother didn't ask questions. Instead they both retreated to their favorite spots in the house, Caroline upstairs in her room, her mother in her chair downstairs. Sam was off somewhere being a boy—playing in the dirt, chasing squirrels, finding mischief. The day seemed to draw out like a thin thread—until the shrill ring of the telephone broke the silence. After a few moments, Mrs. Panski called upstairs.

"Caroline?"

"Yes?"

"The telephone's for you. It's your coach."

Caroline had no idea how to react. She

came down the stairs slowly, and when she entered the kitchen her mother thrust the phone into her hands.

"Hello?" she ventured.

"Hi, Caroline. Listen … we'd like you back. On the team."

She had told him he should be ashamed of himself, told him, his star player, everyone. She had left the building without her stick. As far as she was concerned, she'd quit. And she should stay quit. Was this just another joke anyway, another opportunity to humiliate her? And even if it wasn't, wouldn't it be great to spurn him, show him how it felt?

She heard him sigh and then he said, "Listen. I'm not saying you'll get lots of ice time. But we've got some injuries, you see—two of the guys are gonna be scratched for the next game. Alan, his hamstring. And, well, you keep plugging away, and—who knows? You know?"

"Someone took my stick."

"I suspect I can locate your stick for you."

Caroline looked at her mom. Mrs. Panski nodded at her daughter.

"OK," Caroline said, and hung up.

Mrs. Panski reached out and pulled her into a hug. "I'm proud of you, kid."

Caroline wrapped her arms around her mother's waist. One more chance. She'd make sure it counted.

But there was one more thing she needed to do.

Caroline's old school. It had hardly been a year since she'd been there, but it felt like it belonged to another lifetime. Things had been so much simpler then. She'd had good friends and her dad was still at home and her family was like every other family and her life like any other young girl's in Baltimore. And then her dad had gone off to war and Joseph arrived and her dad died and her friends stopped being friends. It all seemed so long ago.

She walked into the main office. There was someone new working there, a mean looking woman with glasses on a chain around her neck. She seemed annoyed, as if Caroline was keeping her from something important. "Can I help you?" she snapped.

For some reason, Caroline could hardly speak. She muttered and stammered, making the impatient woman even more so. But fortunately, Principal Podolski emerged from his office at that very moment and greeted Caroline warmly.

"Miss Panski, how on earth are you?"

"I'm good, Principal Podolski."

"How is junior high school?"

"It's fine."

"It can be hard. That can be a hard transition."

Caroline nodded.

"Well, what can I do for you?"

"I'm looking for someone."

In his office, the door closed behind them, Principal Podolski rifled through a file cabinet and then pulled out a folder. He opened it and pawed the sheaf of papers inside. "Let's see. Joseph Wilson," he whispered, wetting his thumb with his tongue and flipping through each page. "I have his primary residence as Wolfe Street, but I believe his family moved some months ago."

"Yes," Caroline confirmed. "But I don't know where to."

"I don't have his new address, but as part of our tracking of A-listers and other integraters, we do have notes that he is attending—or at least was attending—St. Peter Claver Church School."

Caroline looked at him blankly.

"It's on the west side. Pennsylvania and … Fremont, I believe. It's a school for Negroes."

Caroline nodded.

Principal Podolski shrugged. "He didn't have an easy time of things here, that's true. I wish I could say differently, but I'd be lying. But I can tell you that you, more than anyone else here, more than even me if I'm being honest, tried to make him welcome. You should be proud of yourself for that."

She thanked him and made her way, via three separate buses, to Pennsylvania Avenue, where she walked six blocks, past the Negro clubs along the strip, northward to Fremont, and entered the St. Peter Claver School.

"Can I help you, miss?" a kindly old gentleman asked Caroline as she wandered the lobby.

"I'm looking for a Joseph Wilson."

The old man looked her up and down a bit suspiciously before he smiled at her. "Well, believe it or not, we have two Joseph Wilsons. I'll fetch them both and you can tell me which is the one you want."

"Thank you."

It wouldn't matter if there were a hundred Joseph Wilsons in that school, of course. She'd know him anywhere. And sure enough, the moment he came around the corner and down the hall toward her, she smiled. And he smiled back. And the "other" Joseph Wilson knew to leave them alone.

"Hi," Caroline said.
"Hi," Joseph replied.

27

COACH HAD BEEN lingering out front, waiting for something. Who knew what? But when Caroline arrived, it seemed that maybe he'd been waiting for her.

She walked from the trolley stop, having made the trip alone. Mrs. Panski had earlier seen her to the stop near their house and told her she'd see her later at the game. "Good luck, sweetheart. Have I told you I'm proud of you?"

"Yes, but thanks."

"Let's go, Panski," Coach said, as she approached. When she got near him, he tilted his head and looked at her long hair, scrunched up in a ponytail. He scrutinized her closely, shaking his head almost imperceptibly, as if already regretting the offer he'd made. But in the end, he held the door for her as she entered. "Third line, second shift. With Reames and Abbott. You got it?"

"Yes, sir," Caroline responded.

He handed Caroline her old beloved stick. She cradled it to her, feeling a bolt of electricity surging up and down her whole body.

"Let's play some hockey," Coach said.

It was a deep and desperate anxiety. Caroline sat alone in the locker room, testing her stick, making sure the tape she'd wound around its length was still holding up. She kicked at her skates, adjusted her pads, expending nervous energy. At moments, she felt like she might throw up. What if she failed out there? What if she got the call and then played terribly? She knew she had to be twice as good, not just okay, to earn continued playing time. This was to be her best shot, and probably her last if she blew it.

She could hear a faint rumble in the building all around her. A wash of noise, nothing discernible, but it seemed to match the rumbling in her stomach. She needed a way to calm down. If she went out there a bundle of nerves, she'd never be able to perform.

And then silence. She couldn't tell if it was her own mind or if something went quiet in the building, but somehow, she managed a shift in that silence. A calm descended on her like a palpable presence. A weighty thing that simply dropped from the ceiling and cloaked her.

She couldn't know that this was the very spot where her mother, playing her own hockey games, had sat many years earlier. She pushed open the door to the locker room and walked into the hall, unaware that this was the very place where Eloise Weatherbee had spoken to Caroline's father for the very first time.

She didn't know that the phantoms of the past are never far, that they float in the filmy memories people carry in their brains and in the collective memory culled from space and time and place. She didn't know that they were there—the ghosts that formed her were right there with her as she snatched up her stick, walked down the hall, and in a sea of calm, joined her team on the bench.

A few odd stares greeted Mrs. Panski as she made her way up the stairs. She returned each one, obviously content to meet them until inevitably the person doing the cowardly staring looked away. "Come on," she said to the boys as they shuffled to their seats.

They settled in and looked around. A good crowd. Not as many as there'd been during Mrs. Panski's playing days, but of course it was a different crowd anyway. Then, it had all been middle-aged men loaded with too much beer and too much testosterone. Today, there were more casual fans and more families, more youngsters, friends, siblings. And there was another thing. Back then, it was an all-white crowd. Today it was almost the same, except for one exception.

"Joseph, are you doing okay?" Mrs. Panski asked.

Joseph nodded, lost in the atmosphere, looking all around him, at the faces, the rink, the teams now spilling onto the ice to perform their skating warm-ups. Mrs. Panski placed a hand on Joseph's shoulder and squeezed slightly. He didn't seem to notice.

What he did, no doubt, notice, what one would have no trouble noticing, was Caroline. One player, and one player only, had a short rope of brown hair tied back into a ponytail that swayed along the shoulders. She circled the lines from goal mouth to midpoint and Joseph watched her every move.

Surely the crowd noticed, too. But just as quickly as the obvious "she" skated her circles, she was back on the bench where she stayed the entire first period. And soon the novelty was gone, subsumed by the action on the ice.

It was a close game, a rare good performance

for Caroline's team. Only 1-0 down at the first intermission, and the crowd was excited about the close game.

"Is Caroline gonna play?" Sam asked.

"I don't know. I don't know," Mrs. Panski answered, anxiousness lacing the edges of her voice. She kept her eyes on the ice, on the bench, on Coach, trying to glean any slight tip-off that her daughter would soon be out there, with her team, taking her rightful place. But she also occasionally cast a glance at Joseph, too, who kept his wide eyes on the rink. He'd told her he'd never seen a hockey game before. Mrs. Panski certainly believed that, even as she still had trouble believing that her daughter had hiked across town, found her old friend, and made him promise to come to her game. Moxie. That's what they called it. So, what could Mrs. Panski do but bring Joseph along to the game?

By the middle of the second period, it was 3-0 with Caroline's team trailing. And still no Caroline.

But with five minutes left in the period, she got the call from the coach and leapt onto the ice.

Mrs. Panski felt a slight pull on her sleeve. "Mrs. Panski, look."

"Mama, it's Caroline," Sam squealed. He stood and pointed.

"I see her. I see her," she said, a smile as broad as any she'd ever smiled stretching across her face. If she or Sam or Joseph had been listening for it, they would have heard, somewhere in the periphery of things, the murmurs in the crowd. Either that was a boy with long hair—simply not possible in this time and place—or, yes, there was a girl out there. There were sniggers, exclamations of disbelief. But to Caroline's mother, brother, and friend, none of that mattered. To them, it felt not like some kind of odd spectacle, but instead like the culmination of something very large and very long in coming. Within the body of that girl on the ice was nothing less than a grand statement, a testament to will and fortitude.

And yet it was just a kid playing a game with other kids. The simplest thing in the world.

Instinct. That was all Caroline needed. She knew how to play. Just let go. Don't think. Ignore the stares, the catcalls, the oafs on the other team mockingly calling her "Sweetheart."

She floated across the surface. The puck knuckled toward her, skipping just over the edge of her stick. It was her first chance at affecting the game, and she'd missed it. She circled back toward the play, watching as the skittering puck that had bounced over the end of her stick was now controlled on the edge of an opponent's wood.

The play moved in the other direction, down ice, the other team putting on the heat, threatening to score again. One of their players wound up, shot, and sizzled it wide, where it caromed around the boards to one of Caroline's teammates, who scooped it out across the blue line.

Caroline sprinted toward center, her stick outstretched before her, ready to receive a pass. She banged her stick on the ice, alerting her teammate to her position. He looked up, saw, and shoveled the puck toward her. It was a weak pass and she had to slow her momentum, digging the heel of her blades into the ice, and cut toward the puck. But doing this stripped her not only of momentum but of balance, too, and as she reached out to meet the puck, one of the boys from the other team disrupted the play. In doing so, he stepped in front of Caroline and sent her tiptoeing across the line as she tried to avoid crashing into him. Her steps mincing and awkward, she fell over and slid headfirst into the boards.

It was one of the odd things about being on the ice, in the middle of the play. All you could hear was the crack of wood on rubber, the bang of stick on ice, the thud of a body careening into the boards. All other sounds melted away into an indistinguishable wash. The hoots and hollers of the spectators were individually indiscernible and instead melded into one low growl. But as Caroline lay there, performing a mental reckoning to assure herself that all her parts were still intact, she could hear the *oohs* and *aahs* of the crowd. As if every single exclamation had funneled through the air and landed, individually, in her ears. She heard the sighs of sympathy and concern, but she also heard the laughter and ridicule, the cowardly outbursts of delight that the girl had gotten what was coming to her.

She picked herself up, determined to shake it off, and slipped back into the flow of the play. The opposing team made a line change, but their timing was poor. They got caught shorthanded and the new line sprinted across the middle trying to catch one of Caroline's teammates speeding down the flank and into the offensive zone. He skipped a pass across the middle, where a lone defenseman poked it out. But he didn't clear the zone. The new line players continued their sprint and clogged the defensive side. The puck bounced around, off sticks, off skates, back and forth, no one in control, until it squirted loose, just to the right of the goal, where Caroline pounced and, without thinking, pulled her stick back and slotted the puck home, lower right corner, past the goaltender's outstretched leg.

The bench erupted. Coach clenched his fist and whistled. "All right, Panski. All right."

Caroline raised her arms in triumph. Her teammates mobbed her, batting her head in that rough affection reserved for athletes playing games of violent poetry.

Caroline looked to the stands, scanning. It wasn't a huge crowd so they were pretty easy to spot. She saw her mom first, standing and shouting, doing little bunny hops in front of her seat. She was wiping tears from her cheeks and smiling, smiling, smiling. There, on either side of her, also smiling and cheering, stood Sam and Joseph. Joseph—he really was here. Back in her life. Caroline waved, and he waved back.

She stared at him and Sam and her mother a bit longer. They continued their cheering and it was only after her teammates had dispersed and the other team had made subs and was getting set to restart, did the head linesman come over. "Okay, little lady. You need to reset," he said. Only then did Caroline finally feel able to move. She took her time heading back to the bench, taking it all in, looking around, seeing the crowd, seeing, again, her friend and her brother and her mother.

And, yes, she was sure of it then, and she'd swear it until the day she died, she saw him also. Her father. Front row, center. Smiling. Winking. Cheering.

You can do anything you want to do, Caroline Panski. Don't ever believe otherwise.

After the game, Coach congratulated Caroline and handed her one of the team sticks. "Good job out there, Panski," he said.

"I can only imagine what you'll be able to do for us with some proper gear."

"Thanks, Coach." She trudged off to the locker room, trailing her two sticks, one in each hand, behind her. She sat by herself on a bench in front of the lockers. It was hard to reflect on anything. Her mind was both a whir of too many thoughts and completely blank at the same time. So she got herself showered and dressed and walked out into the hallway where her mother, Sam, and Joseph stood waiting for her.

"Not bad, sis," Sam said, shaking Caroline's hand. They giggled at the formality of it.

"Thanks," she said.

Mrs. Panski didn't say anything. She couldn't. Her eyes were shining and she blinked back tears of pride. Caroline just smiled at her, everything between them unspoken.

And then there was Joseph, looking shy and out of place.

"Thanks for coming," Caroline said.

"Sure."

Caroline noticed what hung around Joseph's neck. "Nice scarf," she said.

"Oh, yeah. I brought it along to give back." He took it off and handed it to her. "Sorry I had it so long."

"It's okay. In fact," she said, handing it back to him, "I want you to keep it."

"I don't need—"

"Please," she said.

Joseph looked around and then, as if suddenly remembering something, reached into the sleeve of his shirt and pulled a thin piece of rope from his wrist. "Here," he said, handing it to Caroline.

"What is it?"

"It's from South Carolina. Someone gave it to me when I lived there. Well, my daddy did. I know it's just a silly piece of rope, but—"

"I don't think it's silly at all. I love it. But you don't have to give it to me."

"I want you to have it."

Caroline slipped the rope onto her wrist, and then looked up at her friend. "Thank you."

They both stood there awkwardly, no one saying anything. Until finally Mrs. Panski broke the silence. "Oh, go ahead," she said, giving Caroline a slight push toward Joseph.

Caroline leaned in and gave Joseph a big hug.

"Nice game," he muttered.

She just hugged him harder, and this time, he hugged her back.

28

CAROLINE WASHED FOR BED. She was spent, but exhilarated, the events of the day catching up to her. She placed her new stick in the corner of her room, near the closet, next to her pads and skates. It was a solid thing, thicker, heavier, and longer than what she had been using. It would take some getting used to, would probably prove difficult at first. But it was another step in the process and, besides, she worried about her Clippers stick. Just how much more use could it take anyway? She'd noticed the beginnings of a slight crack near the top. Just one more good whack—would it split in half? She couldn't know.

But that wouldn't be an issue. Her mother had a plan.

"Hooks," Mrs. Panski said, holding out her hand.

Caroline handed them over, one at a time.

Mrs. Panski climbed the stepstool and placed the hooks two feet apart and just a foot or so to the right of Caroline's bedroom window, on what had been a big blank space on the wall.

"Hammer."

Caroline handed her mother the hammer, and Mrs. Panski tapped each of the hooks into the wall, tugging a bit on both to test their solidity. Satisfied, she climbed down off the stool. She handed Caroline's stick to her. It was pretty well beaten up. She could see that now, now that it was being retired. Scrapes and scratches decorated both sides from tip to blade. A thick band of tape wound across one section. The Clippers man was still visible, but bits of his beard had been sheared off and he was now missing one of his hands, a small chunk of wood lost somewhere out on the ice. But it was still her stick. All those nicks and scrapes and dings and dents made her smile. In the end, it had held up.

"Go ahead," Mrs. Panski said.

Caroline mounted the stool and placed the stick on the hooks. Then, she took the rope bracelet that Joseph had given her and looped it around the curved end of the stick. She took a step back and admired it, that wonderful stick, which meant so much to her, now retired forever and resting in a place where she'd see it every day. The last thing before going to sleep at night and the first thing when she woke up in the morning.

And there it would stay, the most prominent artifact from a childhood still in bloom but blossoming toward womanhood. A memory, a totem, a reminder and a symbol not only of the good times, but of the loss and the pain and the challenge and the struggle—and how, if we don't give up, we can surmount all of those things.

Acknowledgements

Thanks to the following people: Kristina Makansi, for her editor's eye; my agent, Emily Williamson, for her enthusiasm; and to the inimitable Gilbert Sandler, the new "Sage of Baltimore," for the germ of the idea for *Spitfire* and for taking time on his 90th birthday to talk with me.

About the Author

Evan L. Balkan lives in Towson, Maryland and holds degrees in the humanities from Towson, George Mason, and Johns Hopkins Universities. He is the author of six books of nonfiction, including *The Wrath of God: Lope de Aguirre; Revolutionary of the Americas* (Univ. of New Mexico Press) as well as many essays and short stories. His screenplay *Spitfire,* adapted from the novel, won both the 2016 Baltimore Screenwriters Competition and a Saul Zaentz Innovation Fund Fellowship, and was a semifinalist in the Screencraft Family Friendly Screenplay Competition.His screenplay *Children of Disobedience* won the 2017 Baltimore Screenwriting Competition. He is a co-writer for the television series, *Wayward Girls*. *Spitfire* is his first novel.